This collection is dedicated to the memory of

Olive Charlotte Catherine O'Connor

(1906–1996).

STUBBORN BONES

Karen Smythe.

STUBBORN BONES

KAREN SMYTHE

Polestar Book Publishers
Vancouver

Polestar Books and Raincoast Books gratefully acknowledge the support of the Government of Canada through the Book Publishing Industry Development Program, the Canada Council and the Department of Canadian Heritage. We also acknowledge the assistance of the Province of British Columbia through the British Columbia Arts Council.

Edited by Lynn Henry
Design by Val Speidel
Cover photograph by Bryan Whitney
Author photograph by Ya Ru Yang
Printed and bound in Canada

Earlier versions of the stories were published as follows:
"Stubborn Bones" in the *Antigonish Review*; "The Tooth Fairy, and Other Inventions" in *the Nashwaak Review;* "Dress Rehearsal" in *Fiddlehead*; "The Halfhearted Winner" in *Whetstone*; "Hugging Zero" in *Grain*; "Miss Forbes" (formerly titled "Spinster Alley") in *New Brunswick Reader*; "Stone Haven" in *Antigonish Review;* "Visiting Hours" in *Grain* and in *Water Studies: New Maritime Voices,* ed. Ian Colford (Pottersfield Press, 1998).

The author gratefully acknowledges the support of the Canada Council, which awarded a Literary Arts Development Grant to assist with the completion of this manuscript.

The stories in this collection are works of the imagination, and all characters and events are fictional creations.

National Library of Canada Cataloguing in Publication Data

Smythe, Karen E. (Karen Elizabeth), 1962–
Stubborn bones

ISBN 1-55192-364-5

I. Title.
PS8587.M994S78 2000 C813'.6 C00-910715-0
PR9199.3.S5628S78 2000

POLESTAR, an Imprint of Raincoast Books
9050 Shaughnessy Street
Vancouver, British Columbia
Canada, V6P 6E5
www.raincoast.com

1 2 3 4 5 6 7 8 9 10

Contents

Stubborn Bones

A merry heart doeth good like a medicine:

but a broken spirit drieth the bones.

—Proverbs 17:22

Friday 10 p.m.

Marta's not in mourning, she's in love.

Dressed in a tightly belted blue jersey shift, and wearing sunglasses, she met me at Union Station. She was easy to pick out because of her height—with heels, she is taller than you, remember?—and that waterfalling hair, the colour of corn silk in the sun, could belong to no one else. I expected her to look washed out, weary, at least, but she was smiling as we approached each other. The dark glasses pointed gently upwards at the corners and gave Marta a sly, stylish look. They were not a disguise for sadness.

I felt dowdy, drained, my skin dried by the static air of

the railcar. Marta hugged me close, her long arms cradling me as if I were a doll, and said, "I'm so happy—so happy you are here! I want you to meet him."

At first I thought that she meant to take me to the funeral home, to see her father (whom I'd never met), and that she was still speaking about him in the present tense because he had died so suddenly.

"Dad's best friend has been a *big* help to me."

Ah, so that's it, I thought. I know her codes. I've heard of people making love in cemeteries, but sending perfumed glances over your father as he takes his last breath? Only Marta could displace grief for a gamble; only Marta, from across the hospital bed, could look through the tangle of tubes into the eyes of a stranger and tell him, without speaking, "I wouldn't say no."

You would say I'm being too hard on M., that she should take pleasure where she finds it, why not? You always did. Better sorry than safe, that was your motto. And how many times I heard you say you were sorry! So often that I craved your absence, finally, more than anything in the world. But I used to believe you, gullible girl that I was; I even believed that you really were comforting a broken-hearted Marta one night when I found you embracing on the patio. Yet here I am, going to her, because it seems the right thing to do for such an old friend. Only this time, someone else's husband is comforting dear M.

Saturday Noon

You'd like her apartment. Spare furniture with clean lines and white walls. Sofa a decent enough bed for my well-travelled bones.

M. is in the shower—singing, if you can believe it—but will be ready as soon as she dries her hair. Visitation is this afternoon and I don't know how M. will cope. She hasn't cried yet, at least not in front of me. Marta was not close to him, hardly ever saw her father after her parents divorced; but she was named executor in his will. What a word—as if the dead die again when the remnants of their lives are divvied, disputed, dispersed.

When I was thirteen Father showed me where he kept his will, so I'd know what to do in case the plane he and Mother were taking to Europe were to crash in the Atlantic. As he pulled the envelope from his desk drawer, I was proud and also mortified. It was as though by hinting at death, my parents were inviting it, as though by involving me in the business of dying they were changing my life forever.

At breakfast I asked Marta if she had any unfinished business with her dad. She lifted her face and said, "Jerome and I—it's not a father thing, if that's what you're thinking. I've worked it out. I never even had a father around when I grew up, so how could it be that?"

I looked at our reflections on her black lacquer tabletop, my face stretched out, hers upside down, and I finished my toast. Then she asked after you and I wanted to be gone, anywhere else. I haven't told anyone back home that I left you, and I don't think I want Marta to be the first to know.

Saturday 5 p.m.

At the funeral parlour today, M. greeted visitors with Jerome at her side and I swear it could have been the receiving line at their wedding. Jerome is a little taller than M; he is slight, grey-haired, but has fine features so his face doesn't look his age: it is soft, almost feminine. Reminds me of that actor, you know . . . his name is on the tip of my tongue. Anyhow, they smiled, introduced people to each other, and circulated. "Coffee, anyone?" M. said, barely hiding, barely trying to hide her joy. I avoided Jerome because I didn't want to say, "Pleased to meet you," when I wasn't.

I was glad to leave, around 4 o'clock. There were a lot of people, friends of her father, whose name, by the way, was Henrick. The casket was open. He looked a little like Marta (she looks like him, I should say), and he looked not so much dead as unreal. They had put so much pancake makeup on him—to cover the marks where his head hit the steps, all the way down from the top of the stairs, where his heart stopped—that his face had the sheen of Silly Putty. That colour, too, of new putty before the cartoon ink is picked up and worked through the pinky beige, darkening it.

The whole time we were there I heard the director's adding machine clicking, like a slot machine, in the front office. This is the kind of detail I know you'd appreciate, see the humour in, even.

We came back here to change and M. said, "Come to Jerome's with me. His wife is away and we'll have dinner together." She had her overnight bag in her hand.

Saturday 11 p.m.

We had wine before dinner. Jerome leaned over to refill my glass and then kept his back to Marta while he asked me questions, the first of which was, "What brings you to Toronto?" I thought he must be joking, but he seemed to be serious. I could see Marta's mane behind Jerome's head, a golden backdrop for his performance—not as the best friend, grieving, but the lover.

Because I was bored, I kept imagining his wife would

walk in, a powerful woman bursting in to upend the stage and tear down the scenery. Jerome and Marta were not worried. In fact, they acted as if they were the married couple and even argued over how much wine Jerome had poured for himself while we chatted.

I remember deliberately *not* arguing with you over anything, at first, because I knew you'd just come from a miserable marriage with broken dishes and slammed doors and great silences. I knew you didn't need me, either, and I didn't want to risk moving from shaky ground to a gully.

But later, there were times when I lost my hold and would tell you my fears. Then you would turn away, saying "There are no guarantees," and "It's better this way, we won't go stale." And then I think I hated you, you and your philosophical footwork. I can see myself enraged and devastated—standing in the kitchen, hands gripping the counter, sobbing into the tea-stained sink. All my jealous anger and grief and bruised, untimely love poured out of me. The sight of your back that night was enough to break mine, to break me.

The episode was an excuse for your leaving and you stayed away for weeks. I called Marta only an hour after you were gone. She slept on our sofa for a few days. Then she would leave messages on our machine for me to come home to, so I wouldn't feel so alone in the world. She'd say "Hi, it's me. Just going to sleep so I thought I'd say goodnight," or "Guess you are out. Oh well, I'm thinking of you, sweetie!" or "Call me when you're home. I'll be here!" Things like that. The daily routine of our lives was reported, recorded—shared little reminders that we were important to each other.

Jerome helped to cook the meal tonight. M. donned an apron as soon as we arrived and made herself right at home; and I, in short, did my sociable best throughout dinner. We all seemed so efficient at happiness, and no mention was made of Henrick, none at all. Then M. said, "We'll drive you back." They had done their best, too, and I was in the way. Thirty-two hours on the train, and I was in their way.

Oh, it's late. Too late; now my eyes are heavy but my mind stays awake, and the funeral is at ten in the morning (why are they always morning affairs?). I think I'll change my ticket and leave in the afternoon. Why wait till Tuesday, now? Marta is not alone.

Sunday 3 p.m.

Riding the rails again. I was so eager to climb back aboard today, knowing that I will be home in my own bed tomorrow. I thought of Buster Keaton's "The Railrodder" this morning, his silly slapstick adventure. Hilarious, but *he* never smiles, does he? As he travels down the tracks and across the country, everything he does seems sad and graceful. He tucks a white linen napkin under his bowtie, and the wind blows it upwards, covering his face. In the morning, while the car sways and tilts and bumps along, he manages still to pour, from a silver service into a china cup, his morning tea. Oblivious to weather, to time, to place, he pulls all he needs from a bottomless bin—trying to establish the habits of home, on a moving vehicle, in an unknown land. I always thought that was not so much to ask for, routine. Yet you, my uncharted territory, you resisted such mapping. By me, at least, though invisible ink might have done the trick.

Sunday 10 p.m.

There is something very dismal about underground train stations: entombed, vault-like, gritty as bomb shelters. I can imagine Paris, 1940, desperate people scurrying in the sewers with gunfire around them sounding like knuckles cracking over and over, the echoes hollow and amplified, and bullets sparking off the cement walls.

Remember our honeymoon tour of the catacombs? The humidity suffocated me, tepid water dripping from the lime-lined, too low ceilings with occasional wire-covered bulbs lighting so dimly the slow way down those narrow corridors that seemed to be closing in like a vise. The sign said, in English, "You are now entering the Empire of the Dead"—and then the thick walls of skulls and femurs, arranged in perfect patterns, with signs noting years of plagues and floods and the need for this place, for the undertaker's underworld.

I looked at the millions of bones and thought how willful they are, how stubborn.

It was the usual sermon at Henrick's funeral, about the better world that awaits, and how God takes a life for his own dark reasons sometimes. The minister called him Henry. I sat at the back, in case the service ran late (I didn't want to risk missing my train). Marta sat at the front of the chapel in the family pew with the family few (two cousins, Marta's mother, and her father's aunt). Jerome joined them after the service began. Head high, he glided down the aisle in a sharply pressed grey suit, making a big show of being quiet, and squeezed between M. and the great-aunt, who was too distraught to notice his arrival.

I saw M. turn her eyes from the minister to Jerome, as he approached her. I saw her beam under the broad rim of her black felt hat as she kissed the air with her glossy reddened lips and drew him to her, inhaling deeply.

Monday 11 a.m.

I didn't sleep well last night. First, the blanket the steward gave me was in a plastic bag, and when I took it out I smelled Nan. The nursing home must have laundered its bedclothes in the same institutional detergent, I suppose.

Nan always said she missed my grandfather most when she got into bed at night with the lights off, the sheets cold and crisp. By morning she had used the whole bed, warming it, but waking alone was always a little new, she said, and she never got used to it. I thought I'd be sparing myself such pain, breaking from you before we'd grown old together.

I dozed off and on but was wakened each time we passed through a town—not by the grinding of the brakes, or by the jolts of the engine stopping and starting, but the lights along the tracks were so bright that they pierced the window blind and my eyelids, too. Each time it happened I was confused, thinking I was still at Marta's, but then I would remember that Jerome was probably with her instead.

To energize myself I decided to indulge in a sit-down breakfast. This took courage, because I'm frightened of walking between the cars—those moving pieces of metal, overlapping to make a floating floor, just don't seem stable to me. They remind me of the bends in straws you get in hospitals: jointed like a lobster's claw but, bent too often, they lose their shape and finally break apart.

I ordered one egg, over easy. The package of pepper tore and I spilled so much on the plate that it looked like an ash-tray. That, and the mist outside the window, gave me a sudden craving for the smell of your hair. When we'd shower together the cigarette scent was released by the steam; tiny beads of water would settle on every strand and make you look angel-kissed, unearthly.

If you were here this trip would be exciting. We would dine in the dark on exotic CN fare after the last call. You can make even bologna seem sensuous. Even this scratchy grey blanket would be soft if we shared it—and the rhythm of the train, its blues-call whistle, reminds me of you, too . . .

A woman in her seventies is sitting next to me this trip. Last night, when I really wanted to read myself asleep, I listened to her talk about friends she'd made during her train travels. I had to fake a smile for two hours straight. She smiled too, telling her stories. Smiled through tales of a woman from Vancouver who had become a close friend afterwards, through letters, over the years. Then this friend had written to her asking for help, after a domestic catastrophe of some kind, and she told me—still smiling!—that she never answered, and had thankfully not heard from her since.

"Friendship has its limits," she said, nodding.

You said that our love had its limits, too. Because of me, you said. Because I'm so stubborn and because I would rather be right than happy. Well, my dear, you were dead-on about that, then; but now? Having just done the "right" thing and made no one—not Marta, not myself—happy, I have to wonder what it would be like to meet you again, to try happiness instead of safety.

I can almost see you strutting across the platform to greet me. (You *do* strut, you know! I was always struck by your gallant gait: shoulders braced, arms straight at your side—those solid arms, taut-muscled, thick like clay. You walk with your chest displayed as if adorned with badges of honour won in some distant battle, as if you had inhaled and refused to let go of the breath.)

If only you could read these pages, you would know what my fingers mean should they ever squeeze yours again. Then you would know what my stubborn bones want.

I hear the foghorns in the harbour—like great whale-cries, wired for sound. What power in those subtle bellows, those echoes across the miles, murmured to their own.

Miss Forbes

The week Big Ray proposed, a thick Atlantic fog rolled in and stayed, as if the whole of Lakeside had something to hide. By Wednesday Allie was beginning to feel cranky, smothered by the grey. She loved her mornings, especially at this time of year (the sun was starting to rise a little earlier, day by day), but the wet, clouded air was robbing her of them.

Allie liked to see the sun appear as she looked out the wide end window of her turquoise tin-sided mobile. On clear days she would watch it climb above the scrubby birch branches and evergreens that surrounded the trailer park. Her lot was on a rise and she could pretend she was the only one for miles, if she kept her eyes up and stared out above the rooftops of the others below—trailers with friendly and optimistic brand-names like "Villager" and "Paramount" attached above the hitch, like permanent licence plates. Allie would sip at her tea and listen to her oatmeal bubbling on the stove and stare at the sky and think, "Now *this* is living." And then she'd go to work in Bertha, the '73 Dodge Dart that started like a charm even in February.

Today Allie couldn't see in her rearview mirror the long line of cars she held up as she drove, very slowly, towards Halifax. This morning, like every other of late, she thought about her friend Ray when she rounded a certain bend in Bay Road, because the curve there reminded her of his smile, the snowbanks of the way his whole face was pushed into mounds like doughy dinner rolls when he laughed, which was often. They had some good times together and Allie had grown to need Ray, much as she'd hate to admit it. Ray was the shop teacher at Halifax West. He walked to work from the apartment building where he lived, with a budgie bird, on Ashburn Avenue; walking kept him fit, he said. Ray was a diabetic and weighed 342 pounds.

At the school, after scattering students from the driveway, she parked in her usual spot. They were heading for a cigarette before class on the other side of the walkway, off school property. New rules and they didn't like them one bit, protesting about their rights and such on the six o'clock news. Oh, she'd seen them, posing for the camera with a lit one dangling from a smirk. Flaunting their habit, something Allie couldn't abide. She didn't smoke, never had, though she did try it out once when she was thirteen. She tucked the single cigarette a friend had given her and three matchsticks in her sleeve and walked to the outhouse. Her mother was hanging the wash down the way where the wind blew best, but she had a keen nose and when she passed by she knew. She flung open the door, scaring Allie to death, and then—as if struck—dropped to her knees on the grass and looked up at the sky and asked, right there on the ground, asked the Lord to take her daughter, to take her from the earth if she could not keep herself from sin.

One smoke, then banishment. The next week, Allie was sent all the way to Antigonish, to be saved by the nuns, even though the Forbeses were Baptist. Her father didn't stop it, was probably even grateful, thought Allie much later, since he must have worried that his daughter would one day soon tell on him, tell about those visits to her room when he would lean against the closed door and put his hand down his pants and make her watch. But she didn't tell, had never told anyone to this day, not even Ray ...

Allie wondered if Ray had come in yet. "Ray, Ray, make my day!" She liked to rhyme, to make up little songs in her head. "Little ditties for the little ditzie," that kind of thing. She could say it in her mind but she didn't mean it, it was just a laugh she shared with herself. She was a little different, she knew that. "Unusual," the nuns used to say on those reports they typed up: "Allison is an unusual girl." Something not quite right about her, but nothing anyone could put a finger on, nothing nasty or unclean.

She watched for black ice on the bare, wet pavement, counting the gasoline rainbows she saw underfoot on the way to the door. To her side, she hugged her vinyl purse. Pretty light, she thought, counting up in her head what was in it: two lipsticks (one spare), some half-used Kleenex, a leather pouch with her driver's licence and some lunch money. As she went she tried to breathe as little as possible, hold her breath, even. Not because of the air, fume-filled from rush-hour buses and trucks, but so she wouldn't soak up the voices of the kids, laughing and swearing and being rude out there in the blue morning cold with traffic zipping by them where they stood, inches from the curb.

Sometimes they teased Allie. They did. One boy would say, in a grade-school way, "Miss Forbes! Good morning, Miss Forbes. And how is Miss Forbes today?" Another said one time, "Hey, good looking!" and when she turned he said, "Can't you take a joke?" Now she counted the rainbows or cracks in the asphalt or whatever else she saw on the ground, as long as she didn't let them see her eyes.

She hung up her coat and unwrapped her head, wound round and round with the pink chiffon scarf Ray had given her for Christmas. He must have noticed that her hair was thinning but he would never say anything. When they exchanged Christmas presents at Allie's place this year, Allie was glad to see the pink scarf in its white tissue paper because she wasn't prepared for more than that. She knew Ray had a soft spot for her but she wasn't sure what he planned to do about it. As for buying his gift, her shopping was easy. She put some plastic toys for his bird in Ray's stocking and hung some diabetic candy canes from the edge of the kitchen counter—Allie didn't have a fireplace, of course, not in a trailer. She also boxed up a gift certificate to Kent's. Ray could pick out some wood for any project he wanted to make, she figured, but when he saw the coupon he said he'd use it to build a fake fireplace for her. He had found, at a yard sale last summer, plastic logs that glow when you plug them in, and they'd be perfect, he said, for under the mantel. The blinking green lights Allie had trailed around the window frame flashed on and off behind Big

Ray's face as he told her his idea, and she thought he looked like an angel.

In the office Heather sat at Reception with some tissue balled up against her red nose. Swollen eyes with rings under them, coloured like the gasoline in the parking lot, and no makeup. Not the usual perky gal at all.

"Heather, is that you?" Allie tried to make her smile, forget herself. Best way to get over little difficulties that can seem the world, that's what she had to remember all the time and she figured Heather could benefit from her wisdom, too.

But Heather didn't smile, she bawled instead and blurted her story to Allie as if she were the best confidante she'd ever had.

"My ring's gone and Kevin says I'm too stupid to marry because if that's how much I care about the ring then I couldn't give a shit about him either and it's all my fault and it's over, but it's not my fault, I loved that ring just like I love Kevvie but it fell off in my glove 'cause I was so cold and my fingers shrink when they're cold and I was helping him fix his truck last night 'cause he was going to the bar and the truck wouldn't start 'cause it was freezing out so I was holding the flashlight for him so he could pour in that antifreeze goop and when he got her going and took off I went back in and took my glove off, and the dumb acrylic things don't keep you warm anyways, I don't know why I bother wearing them, but the ring must've got caught on the threads and got flung off somewheres in the lobby and no one has turned it in of course, would you if you found a diamond ring lying there, even if it is a small one and just made of them cheap little chips, still it was mine and I loved it and now Kevvie won't even talk to me!"

Couldn't get a word in, most likely, thought Allie, though she always said Kevvie sounded like a real prize, oh yes, the way he was always broke and bossing Heather about; and he was going to make her quit work once they were wed, too, even if all they had was pogey to live on. But that was before and now that he wasn't going to go through with it, he couldn't force her to do anything, could he? Silly girl.

Allie would never quit her job typing at the school no matter how unkind the students and no matter who might think she should. It was her living, her independence. It let her stay cheaply in her trailer and enjoy some happiness of her own, and she could afford to buy skeins of yarn for her knitted dishcloths (China Rose and Raspberry were the colours she would try next). It let her keep Bertha on the road, too. She thought of herself as a career gal, because she had a job she could wear dresses to every day of the week. She'd found a niche here (nitch, she called it), at the school and in the park, and even went so far as to belong to Beechville Baptist—mostly for the fun of going to teas and setting up in malls with bake-sale tables. (Once a month, as a favour to Reverend Percy, Allie prepared communion for a congregation of sixty-three, slicing the stacked bread into bite-sized squares with an electric knife and squirting a taste of grape juice into each crystal mini-cup, using a syringe Ray had given her from his insulin supplies.)

All of it, this life she loved, was possible because she'd learned to type. When she was with the nuns she copied down the rows of letters on Sister Donna's machine and practised on her pillow at night. She imagined that she was playing an instrument, that each tap tap tap was a musical note that made memorizing easier because all she had to do was sing a tune in her mind to remember the letters as she went along.

"I typed myself out of that place," Allie told Ray when they were having lunch in the cafeteria one day, "out of that school and into this one. I guess I owe my mother for an education after all!" Ray was enjoying the fish-and-chip special that day. He stabbed the breaded cod with his fork and said, "Allie, we all gotta count our blessings, don't we? You know what I mean. Not religion-wise, that's not it. But take us, for example. You and me. I'm glad to know you, real glad. We care about each other. That's what counts."

Heather was still sniffling so Allie made a mug of tea for her with the kettle they kept in the staff washroom, next to the principal's office. When students were given the what-for by Mr. Lowes in there, she would sometimes go in and close the door to listen through the wall with the lights out. Allie felt like she was in a confessional box, the cool tiles of the wall against her ear vibrating with Mr. Lowes's proclamations. As the tea steeped she looked at herself in the brown-spotted mirror and rubbed her lips together to even out her lipstick. Who's the fairest of them all? Allie smiled because she wasn't fair in the least. She had had dark hair when she was young, and now she dyed it whatever brown was on sale every six weeks.

She took the cup to Heather's desk, where it sat cooling. Big Ray came in just then. He took one look at Heather, who had finally stopped crying but was rubbing her ring finger as if it were a rabbit's foot, and turned to Allie. She mouthed the name "Kevvie" and fed a sheet of foolscap into the IBM Selectra so that Ray could take over.

"What's the problem?" he asked. "There's nothing I can't fix but the crack of dawn, you know."

Heather always laughed behind Ray's back but she told him the story anyway, slower this time, and by the end of it Ray was promising to help her look for the missing gem at the end of the day. Allie pictured his bulk bent down on the carpet of Heather's lobby, looking for the tiny ring, rapping on doors and asking the neighbours if they'd seen it. She smiled and thought if anyone could find it, or get a person to admit they'd picked it up, it was Ray. He could probably fix the crack of dawn, too, if he had his heart set on it.

When Allie started to lose her hair, she would count the strands that came free in her fingers as she showered. When there were too many to keep track of she'd gather them all up by rubbing her hands together in a circle, making a knot, and then she'd paste the wet nest to her chest so it wouldn't clog the drain. She knew it was "the change" and had something to do with hormones, but she tried not to think about getting old and going bald. She always took care to wear scarves, like the one Ray gave her. As if she were Grace Kelly of Monaco instead of Allie Forbes of Lakeside, Nova Scotia.

Now she was getting ready for church. Today was just a regular service ("No Christ-cutting to be done, doo-dah, doo-dah," she hummed), so she could take her time. She stood under the water until she was all warmed up; the steam in the shower stall was so thick that she could no longer see the green-grey mildew in the grouting. That mess would have to be cleaned up, first, then covered up with Liquid Paper from the office. She would have to bring a new bottle home with her on Monday night. "L.P., L.P., L.P., L.P.," she typed on her thigh to remind herself.

As she turned the water off she sang the same tune she always sang in the shower: "I am slowly going crazy, One Two Three Four Five Six—Switch!"

Allie knew she wasn't crazy, though, and she knew she wasn't wicked, no matter what her mother or Sister Donna always said. Forgetting was just her trick.

Because life, sometimes, could be a bit much.

"Just too much," said Allie, clasping the brunette-tinted ball of hair and dripping onto the brown marble-patterned linoleum floor that should be cleaned, she thought, before the start of another week. She'd cleaned herself, at least, could still taste the faint sweetness of the Ivory suds that had got on her lips from the facecloth. She'd grown to like the flavour, which she knew was strange, because it took her back each time to her mother's fingers and the soap against her teeth, her rough fingers shoving the sliver in and out of her mouth. Oh my god yes.

She watched as each splash that fell from her hit the floor. Little rivers collected lint and loose flecks of fibre and hair and skin (and hair—so much hair!), and carried them away from Allie's bony toes. She stayed there a long time. What she thought about, as she stood there, shivering, had nothing to do with her youth. No, what she thought about, that Sunday morning in the bathroom, was Ray asking her to marry him.

This is how it happened: he did find Heather's ring on Thursday night, and the girl hugged him, laughing, after he slid it on her finger. Ray told Allie about it on Friday, demonstrating it all with a ring he had bought at People's Jewellers on his way home. He held her hand and put the ring on (it was loose, but he promised to have it sized later) and then, as if it weren't weeks after Valentine's Day, said, "Allie Forbes, be mine."

Well . . . ?

She hadn't given a thought to the intimacies at all—never had. Men had never interested Allie, not in that way; one of her unusuals, that was how she would explain it to Ray, though of course she knew the reason. And much as Allie loved Ray, he was like the best girlfriend she'd always wanted. Besides, they were too old for that foolishness! They were no Heather and Kevvie! No, nights were out. But if they were to share their days, which was what Ray might have in mind as well ...? Allie imagined that she'd have to sell Bertha and move to Ray's or else he'd have to come live in the trailer court and the extra strain on Bertha's suspension during the rides to school and back every day would put her to an early death. Either way there was the budgie to contend with, the bird that said "Pretty boy, pretty boy" all day long, and that would drive Allie over the edge, she was sure of that.

See? She was too set; she couldn't live with anyone. She didn't deserve Ray, she thought sadly. Diabetic or not, he needed someone sweeter than Allie could ever be.

She dried her legs and picked out the clothes she would wear to church: a navy skirt with a red sweater, and a red scarf to match, tied around her hair. She pulled a fringe of bangs down on her forehead and powdered her face with cornstarch, a cost-saver she'd heard about on the radio once. When she was done she looked at herself, pleased. Even her lazy eye seemed straighter.

Yet Allie was flustered. She fumbled with the clasp of her imitation pearls behind her neck. She couldn't get the necklace done up, so she dropped it into a dish on the dresser. The proposal, the change it meant—even if she said "No"—was going to rattle things, and change her. She was trying to forget herself, but Ray wouldn't let her! He was waiting for her answer, said he'd waited this long to have somebody and he could wait a little longer, if time was what Allie needed. Was that what she needed? she wondered. Time?

As she stared in the mirror a single strand of hair dropped from her head, and Allie felt it come to rest on top of her left hand. She looked down and saw it was pointing like a fine arrow to the finger Ray's ring would soon fit.

Allie was crying now. She was falling apart, and she felt like she was losing more than just her hair. And yet Ray loved her. He said he even loved the way her eye rolled to the side when she looked at him, because it made him think she knew some secret about him that pleased her. He loved her, and because of that Allie didn't know if she could ever forget herself again.

"Don't be so foolish! Pull yourself together, Miss Forbes," she said to her reflection, imitating Sister Donna. She dabbed her eyes with a new tissue, then put on her muskrat coat, which made her feel like a million. Then she went outside to start the car.

It was a bright day and Allie noticed that the rust eating ragged brown frowns into Bertha's body had gotten worse this winter. She sighed. She knew the day was coming when Bertha would have to go to the scrap heap. This saddened her more so she tried not to think about it.

Bertha started up fine but when Allie backed out of the driveway, the car choked and then stalled for the first time that she could remember. “What are you trying to tell me?” she said. She sat there a minute, took some deep breaths, and watched the windows steam up. She tried again. The motor whined and whirred, but would not turn over.

Allie knew Ray would be there in a flash, somehow, if she were to go back inside and call him. Not that he knew much about cars, but he’d find a way to help, to get her to church on time. Then again, maybe this was her cue to skip all that, to call Ray and tell him she had made up her mind . . .

She had almost given up hope when the engine caught, and she was off.

The Tooth Fairy and Other Inventions

The war against the fleas had been raging for a week, and everyone was miserable—except for David, for whom a problem, any problem, is an opportunity to shine. He'd been spraying our rugs every day, every inch, up and down. This is good, if you're the kind of person who, like me, does not want to spray rugs up and down, especially at six in the morning.

I stood in damp stockings (I'd forgotten my slippers again) and watched as he poured the bottle the vet had given us onto a plate, dipped a comb into it, and ran the wet teeth against the grain of our puppy's golden fur. Chester scratched his side with a hind foot, as if he wanted to direct David's attention there.

"Aha! Found another one!"

"I don't think it's true, what people say about you."

"What? What do they say?"

"They say, 'That David, he wouldn't hurt a fly.'"

"Hey," he said, laughing, "as soon as I finish the morning kill here, I'll make you some pancakes." I saw a bowl of batter he'd already mixed and set aside to rise. I thought, *David is too good to be true.*

"I'm meeting Andrea today," I reminded him, "so you don't need to pack me a sandwich."

When Ingelore's daughter called and asked me to meet her for lunch, I tried to say that I had too much work to do, couldn't get away from the office all week. But I couldn't summon the effort to make it believable.

"I may stay late to catch up on the accounts," I told David. "I can pick up some take-out for dinner, if you don't mind waiting for supper till I get home."

"Don't worry about it, sweetheart," he answered. "I can fend for myself."

"I know you can. It's just me we have to worry about." For years, until David moved in with me and took over the cooking, I had been on a coffee-and-Kraft-Dinner kind of diet, which had always disgusted my mother. Once, David called her and told her we having Clark's beans for dinner, right out of the can, and asked if she wanted to join us. When I frowned, he said, "Oh come on! You've got to have some fun with her once in a while," and I had to smile at that.

David served my breakfast and sat down at the table. "I can't imagine why Andrea wants to see me," I said between bites. "It's really strange that she tracked me down after nearly two years, don't you think?"

"Maybe she takes after Ingelore," David said. "Maybe she's a little bit, you know—off."

David and I moved into a new apartment the summer that Ingelore went crazy—which is how my mother refers to that summer, still, using Ingelore the way that some people use natural disasters or wars, as a way of marking time. When we had been unpacked for a month or so Mother called, and I was telling her about the view we had from the balcony and about the container garden I couldn't keep alive out there, but she wasn't listening.

"Ingelore's gone away again," she said, making it sound like an extended vacation. Ingelore had, in fact, checked herself into a private psychiatric clinic downtown.

"That's really a shame," I said, and I meant it. "Are you going to visit her? I could go with you—"

"Oh my goodness, no," she said, speaking very quickly. "No no no! If she wants visitors she'll call. Anyhow. It's raining here. What's it doing where you are?"—as if we lived in different countries, not a fifteen-minute drive away.

After we hung up I couldn't stop thinking about Ingelore. She used to come over to visit my mother once or twice a week when I was growing up. When I'd get home (we lived across the street from the school), she always smiled and walked towards me, then held her arms wide. "How's my girl?" she'd ask, holding me against her for a few seconds longer than seemed necessary. I think she felt sorry for my mother, and for me, because my father (who had been a friend of her husband Larry) left us and moved to California when I was nine years old. I thought that was why Ingelore visited so often, anyway. My arrival was her cue to pick up her own kids, Andrea and an older boy, Robert, and so I never spent much time with her. But the house felt different on days when she'd been there.

Once, at lunch time, Ingelore came in without ringing the doorbell, bringing waves of fresh air with her. It was the day after my grandfather died, and I was home from school to help by keeping my grandmother company. The garlic and oregano of a warm lasagna suddenly filled the living room.

"You poor thing, I am so, so sorry," she said, crouching at Grandmother's knee. "It's a good thing you're with your family right now. I'm glad this sweet girl is here with you."

My grandmother, stunned by grief, didn't know what to say to this woman she didn't know, this woman who stood before her with real sorrow on her face.

Mother took the foil pan, saying, "Ingelore, you shouldn't have!" in the same voice I'd heard her use two weeks ago when a blind date—somebody's single cousin, brought along to balance the numbers at the dinner table—gave her a bottle of wine. "Let's sit in the kitchen," she said to her friend. "I've just made a pot of tea."

I sat back down next to my grandmother and held her hand. "Ingelore is a good friend of Mother's." She nodded and leaned against the sofa, her eyes closed, and within a few seconds she was wheezing through her mouth, sleeping. I couldn't hear anything from the other room, so I went to the hallway and peeked around the corner.

"Losing a parent is awful, at any age. Awful," Ingelore repeated, looking intently at my mother as she spoke. Mother's lips were pursed so tightly that they had almost disappeared. Moving very slowly, she put her cup on the table and left her hand there, hovering on its edge. Ingelore stood up and went to her. She put her arms around Mother's shoulders and looked, it seemed to me then, like an older sister, like someone who might give solid advice on hair colour, hem lengths, love.

At first I didn't recognize Andrea, who was waiting for me at the restaurant. Her long black hair hung limp and untended instead of curled to perfection, as it used to be. When we were teenagers, her face constantly beamed as though she had just won a beauty contest, which she easily could have; she was the kind of girl who wore a permanent smile and always had boyfriends, and other boys following her around, waiting for their chance. We had nothing in common, though we were expected to get along because we were in the same class and because our mothers knew each other so well. I hadn't seen her since the funeral.

"How are you, Andrea?" I said as I joined her.

"Fine, thanks."

And I'm the tooth fairy, I thought. She had already finished her wine and poured more from the carafe, then filled my glass.

"I hear you've tied the knot," she said.

"That's right, I did. Last summer. It was just a small ceremony," I added, aware of the chance that Andrea may have felt slighted (she'd invited me to hers, or Ingelore had, but I didn't go). "My husband's name is David. He just started his own desktop publishing company—he runs it from our house." Andrea seemed not to be listening, but I continued to talk about my work, our house, our dog. "We have a flea problem these days, I'm afraid."

"Fleas? Oh, your dog—your dog has fleas."

I had run out of small talk. I noticed that she was not wearing a wedding ring, but I didn't want to ask her about that. "Is there something on your mind, Andrea? I mean, was there something you wanted to see me about?"

"Yes. I'm sorry. Yes, there is. Look—did you know my father is marrying her? You know, the woman he started seeing before my mother—before she died?"

"Oh," I said, "I'm sorry. But I—no, I didn't know."

"I didn't even know it was going on, until after. You must have known, didn't you?"

I was thinking of the time Mother told about some blonde—Larry's fiancée, now—who had been at one of their sets' parties. She said Larry spent the evening with her, ignoring Ingelore, while everyone pretended that there was nothing going on.

"You don't have to answer that," she said. "The point is, I knew nothing. Nothing about her, or the marriage, or my mother. I never asked her anything personal—I never really *talked* to her, you know? Not really, not about anything real ..." She looked down at her plate, at the food she had barely touched. Then she looked up at me. "She spent time around you, at your place. Tell me something about my mother."

Andrea was haunted; of course she was. It's all in the afterwards, I thought—in the words after, the saying and not saying, making someone up so you can know them. Know them, and forget them.

So I told Andrea that her mother had warmed our mournful house one afternoon with her homemade lasagna and with an embrace that reached my mother when I didn't even know that such a gesture was possible, let alone the most necessary of acts.

I left work early that afternoon, even though I was behind in my financial statements. As I drove I thought about the things Andrea had said about her parents' marriage. My mother had told me that Ingelore would never leave Larry, because of her belief. "She's Catholic, that's why. Divorce just isn't part of their vocabulary. Besides, in our day, when your father gave you away you were married for life. Not really knowing your husband all that well before the wedding was part of the fantasy." She smiled then as if she could see herself at the altar, as if time had stopped at that moment and the rest of her life had not happened to her.

I had gone to the visitation with Mother, of course. When we arrived Andrea was not there yet, or she had already been and gone. We stood listening to Larry explain why Ingelore was going to be denied the rites of Catholic burial.

"Ingelore knew before she took those pills that she wouldn't be put in sacred ground. The embarrassment she's caused the family. Not to mention our priest, for Christ's sake!"

Mother—who the day before had sworn that she hated Larry with all her might—was standing next to him, and she touched his elbow. "I know, Larry, I know. You must be suffering. *Enormously*."

I looked up at the wall above the closed casket at the end of the sunny room. I thought I could make out a winged image made of blues and greens and yellows, though the funeral home was secular and I knew that there was no such thing there, that it was really just a mirage made by shafts of light prismed through a dirty bevelled window.

When I got home I was careful to stay out of David's way. While he discussed a project with a client in his office downstairs, I crept up our narrow staircase to lie down. Chester barked, then followed me. David heard the noise and popped his head out the door.

"What are you doing home? Are you all right?"

"I'm fine. Just a headache," I assured him over my shoulder. "I shouldn't have had wine with lunch, that's all. I'll tell you about it later."

Upstairs I started to undress but managed to take off only my blouse before I felt dizzy. I lay on my back across the bed and moved my straightened arms up and down at my side, as if I was making a snow angel, until the feeling went away.

I turned on the small second TV we keep in the bedroom for the times that insomnia strikes one of us. Daytime programs were unknown territory for me, so I changed channels until I heard a familiar, calming voice: it was Gloria Steinem, on a talk show promoting her newest book. She wore a black miniskirt and a loose-fitting white top, and she looked elegant and much younger than I knew she must be.

"Self-esteem is the biggest problem in the world," she was saying. "People who lack it either lash out at others or else they self-destruct. I don't have to tell you which way women turn most of the time."

Chester whimpered and jumped up on the bed. He knew he wasn't allowed up there, but I didn't have the heart to push him off.

The show was over. During the applause, credits began to roll and a deep male voice announced, "This broadcast was brought to you by Revlon. The most unforgettable women in the world wear Revlon. Beautiful!"

I turned off the television and stared at the screen while Gloria's image, like a luminous ghost, seemed to pulse for a moment before it faded and disappeared.

I tried to picture the look on Andrea's face after we said goodbye and I turned away. I knew she wanted me to keep talking, and that it wouldn't have mattered what I said, or if I made up all kinds of things; not as long as I kept going. But I didn't. Outside the restaurant we shook hands and she thanked me for coming. That was when I could have said, "I know you're in trouble. You can talk to me." I could have taken her phone number and said, "I'll call you." But I am my mother's daughter, and all I said was, "Take care of yourself, Andrea." Then I checked my watch, and walked away.

Chester squirmed beside me. He had settled in for a

deep sleep and, I supposed, happy dreams. The bedding would have to be stripped, of course, but I knew David wouldn't mind that I'd broken the rules.

"He'll take care of us, Chester," I said, petting his head. "We'll be just fine. Won't we, now?"

Dress Rehearsal

Leilah was sprawled on the sofa, trying to remember when she had lost all interest in sex, when the phone rang. It was Scott, her landlord. He lived with his lover, Steven, on the first floor of the house; a single mother with her four-year-old lived on the third. Leilah and her husband lived in between.

Leilah had been married to Colden for three years now, but the buzz had worn off after two. She once told Scott it felt like she'd stayed awake too long after drinking a bottle of better red wine. She and Scott had become close over the years, spending mornings together over frothy lattes in his kitchen before going to their part-time jobs in the afternoon. Scott was a case worker at the Toronto Children's

Aid Society; Leilah was a receptionist at a PR firm, and had been hired mainly for her looks.

Scott made Leilah laugh a lot during these chats, which she needed. Colden was a talker, but not a listener. Sometimes when Leilah talked he would stare at her, waiting for her to get to the point, and she'd say, "I guess that wasn't a very interesting story," and then he'd laugh, which she knew was his way of forgiving her.

"Leilah, doll," Scott said, "my Filter Queen has abdicated, stepped down from the throne—in other words, conked out."

"You've worn it out, is more like it," Leilah said, "but not to worry. I'll bring my lower-ranking servant down for you."

Taking her Hoover from the closet, Leilah noticed smudges of brown grime around its boxy yellow body.

"Scott probably *vacuums* his vacuum. I can't hand this over to him," she said out loud, though she was alone. Her insecurity had reached new heights—or depths, she thought, as she reached under the kitchen sink for a clean J-cloth. Her friends used to think it was put on, that someone as attractive as Leilah could not possibly lack confidence, but she was never completely comfortable with her beauty. She suspected that she would wake up one day to find that it had evaporated overnight, good bone structure and all. Beauty was random and transitory. She was bright enough to know that, even if her friends wouldn't admit it.

Leilah didn't have many friends left, at least not many she cared to see much of anymore. Those from her pre-Colden, college days had drifted into the suburban lifestyle they once had mocked. Now they spoke as though their twenties had been some sort of dress rehearsal for real life—as if Leilah would discover that herself, if she and Colden ever decided to stop living like a couple of students. "If you ever grow up and have kids" was what they meant. These friends sent Leilah Christmas cards with form-letter summaries of children's accomplishments and family vacations, photo postcards of infants on Santa's knee. Even the husbands Leilah used to flirt with out of habit talked of mortgages and day care at their dwindling get-togethers, which Colden boycotted. They had started to bore her, too, these dinners and brunches, but lately they had become even worse than that. Lately Leilah felt a heaviness in her chest whenever she spent time with the old crowd.

After she had wiped down the vacuum and replaced the bag (just in case Scott was to look), she glanced into the next room. She should do some cleaning herself, she thought, noticing the grey dust-clouds held together by hairy threads that circled the legs of the scratched mahogany dining table.

She and Colden had bought the antique as a wedding gift to themselves, but when they'd gotten it home they realized it wasn't in the best of shape. Leilah was distracted from the memory of their disappointment when the boy upstairs began jumping off the furniture.

"Knock it off!" she half shouted through clenched teeth—at the boy's mother more than at the boy. Leilah used to complain to her that she feared for her china, but it hadn't done any good. "If you had any kids of your own," the woman had said, "you'd understand."

She put on some coral-coloured lipstick, the only make-up she ever used or needed: her skin was so flawless it could have been air-brushed, as Colden put it. This was quite a compliment, she knew, especially since Colden worked for an advertising agency and was around perfect-looking people all day long.

She draped the vacuum hose around her neck and headed downstairs. When Scott opened the door, she said, "I'll have you know that this machine is circa 5 B.C. Before Colden, that is."

Scott laughed as he hung the hose on the brass coat stand inside his foyer.

"Some neighbours ask for a cup of sugar. But not you, Scott."

"Well, landlords can be pushier, you know."

Leilah followed him into his kitchen. "Next you'll be asking for my first born."

Scott looked at her from under lifted eyebrows as he filled his chrome-and-black kettle at a sink that shone, Leilah noted, like a showroom model.

"No, I am not pregnant," she responded when she realized what he was thinking. Once, she told Scott when her period was late, the automatic panic left over from her dating years spilling into her married life because she and Colden had not talked about being parents. Until then, she had never seriously asked herself if she wanted children. She'd always assumed it would happen one day, but Colden was definitely not ready. He had said, when she asked him, "Why rush into all of *that*?" as if he'd bitten into a sour apple. That crisis was some months ago now, and she hadn't let herself think much about it since.

"Hey, you have new dishes!" Bone-white mugs were displayed at eye level on an open shelf. They formed a semicircle and looked like six perfectly shaped porcelain teeth, grinning at her.

"Steven felt like a change. They're not what *I'd* have chosen, but I'm learning to compromise, apparently."

"So what else is new with you? How's work these days?"

"Last week was tough. We had a ten-year-old boy on drugs. Ten! His mother—you know the type. She slicks her hair back with margarine instead of mousse."

Leilah didn't know what Scott was talking about. What kind of woman would butter her head? "I can't imagine doing your job, Scottie. I'd be so depressed all of the time."

"And you're *so* happy now, is that it? Hey, wait a minute—did you say 'Scottie'? No one has called me that since I was five. It makes me feel like a dog!" and he gave a little bark. "Scottie the Terrier ... I kind of like it."

"Colden says most men are just like dogs, when you come right down to it. They want nothing more than a bitch in heat and a meaty bone, and not necessarily in that order."

"In that case, I guess I don't qualify as man *or* dog, according to Colden's standards." Leilah knew Scott didn't like her husband very much and she couldn't blame him. Colden hardly ever spoke to Scott or Steven.

"What's the Golden Boy up to today?"

"He's playing squash with Derek," Leilah said. "Same routine every Saturday, rain or shine."

"Ah, the male code. I've heard of it."

"Exactly. Winning is a matter of honour with those two, like dueling or something. He goes off to defend his title and leaves me to the housework. Plus he hates it when

I'm possessive, and he says spending time apart helps hold a marriage together."

"Oh no. It isn't falling apart again, is it?" Scott couldn't take anything Colden said seriously. And normally Leilah would have a comeback, but today the question slapped her hard, and her eyes burned.

"Can I ask you something, Scott?"

He put his arm around her shoulders and led her to the living room. They sat side-by-side on Scott's green leather couch.

"Here it is. Yesterday, Colden's boss, Marianne, confided in him at the agency. About something . . . personal."

"And?"

"And—well, I've been thinking about it. A lot. Because this kind of thing you don't tell someone, especially not your employee, unless you want to move the relationship to—well, to a certain level of intimacy. Colden shouldn't know this about his boss." Leilah saw her face reflected in Scott's glasses, her mouth distorted and ugly. She looked away and drank from her mug, leaving a veined plum stain on its rim.

"Leilah honey, what did she tell him?"

"Her husband has left her. For another man."

Though Leilah checked his face for surprise, Scott's

expression remained steady. His elbows were on his knees, chin resting on index fingers that made an inverted V, reminding Leilah of the child's hand-game that began, *Here's the church, here's the steeple.*

"You know," Scott began in a low, gentle voice, "I think you must be bored, Leilah. I mean, where is this coming from?"

"Don't you think . . . it would make anyone think . . . well, you wonder about their love-life, about what went on in the marriage, don't you, after hearing that?" Leilah's voice was rising higher and higher. She hated the sound of herself, and at the same time she was annoyed that Scott didn't immediately agree with her, see her point of view, commiserate.

"I doubt that Colden is going to look at her that way all of a sudden, if he hasn't before. Besides, since we're in the dog motif today, you could say Colden is as domesticated as a poodle. He may be a silly man, but he's definitely *your* man. I don't have to tell you that. Now, what's *really* bothering you?"

Leilah laughed a little, and shook her head. "I don't know."

After leaving Scott to his housecleaning, Leilah gathered the week's washables into a canvas carry-all and headed to the laundromat. Between stations the subway crawled from the tunnel and the surprise of the sun made her shrink back and turn her head away from the window for a moment. As her eyes adjusted to the light, she watched a middle-aged man's face come into focus at Rosedale. He had short silver hair, side-parted like her father's had been, and he wore an expensive-looking suit with a red tie. When the doors slid open, clunking like a prison gate, Leilah saw that the man's navy blazer topped a straight, knee-length, grey flannel skirt. He wore pumps that matched both his tie and his very faintly pencilled-in lips. Leilah felt as though she were at a magic show, but instead of seeing a female assistant sawn in half, she saw two people joined together in an instant.

The man found a seat and crossed his legs. Leilah had looked away when she had first seen him get on, but she still could see from the corner of her eye a red shoe bobbing up and down with the jerky motion of the train. She noticed a wedding ring on his left hand as she stood up at her stop. As she began to climb the stairs to the street, her light laundry bag slung over her shoulder the way male models carry a raincoat in fashion magazines, the silver-headed mystery man was sped away.

Leilah wondered about him as she separated the whites from the colours and loaded the machines with quarters and detergent. Saturday, she thought, must be his day for dressing up. Images of the man sitting on a bed—pulling on panty hose and slipping into a skirt while his wife made scrambled eggs downstairs—spun round her mind as she watched familiar blue socks tumble in the heavy-duty dryer. Did his wife desire him? Did she enjoy him, in those clothes? Or did the woman wait in a twin bed for his attentions, and have trouble sleeping when he disappointed her? Did he go through the motions, now and then? Maybe his wife was relieved, not having to perform any wifely duties at this point in her life. Maybe she was completely satisfied with her existence, and was happy to scramble eggs, wash the dishes, maintain a household, play bridge with her friends. But somehow, even if his marriage was passionless, she doubted that this fellow would want a real man to touch him. She thought it was probably the idea of being looked at that thrilled him. She decided she'd ask Scott for his opinion on that one, next time they talked.

Sometimes when Leilah was alone with Scott she wondered if he had ever looked at her sexually and been disgusted. She thought she understood why some men prefer male lovers, because she could easily be ashamed of her own subtle body odours, of her secretions, her hormones, her messy cycle and sticky arousals. Though Colden revelled in it all. He still urged her to "go natural," to give up deodorant even, since he loved the way women smell. She remembered that at dinner with Derek and Shelley last month (or was it the month before?), Colden had talked about an idea for a new perfume commercial he wanted to pitch to his colleagues at the firm.

"It would be a celebrity spot. We'd get Al Pacino to say, 'The scent of a woman—yes, it *can* be bottled!'" Everyone had laughed, except for Leilah, who thought the joke was vulgar. They'd argued about it when they got home, and Colden—afraid that the other tenants might hear them—hushed Leilah as he rushed around the flat closing windows, which made her want to scream.

A few days after that evening, Derek and Shelley split up. Leilah realized that she'd not told Scott this news, or the reason for it. "Shelley's clock is ticking and Derek's not ready for that. He's like us," Colden had explained to her. In response Leilah had said nothing. Later that night they made love, she remembered, but she had had trouble relaxing; afterwards she stared at the small piece of white lint in Colden's bellybutton as he fell asleep.

"Lint," Leilah murmured to herself, remembering to pull the screen from the dryer. She peeled the soft, warm blanket from the mesh, wondering how so many fibres could come loose from the clothes each time they were washed without you noticing that anything was missing.

She left the sheets in a pile with the rest of the clean clothes when she got home and stretched out on the bare mattress in the bedroom, resting her hands on her abdomen. Her tummy was still taut and firm, free of the postnatal stretch marks her friends boasted. Somehow its smoothness had become strange to her.

Not so long ago Leilah used to enjoy her body. There had been so many nights when she was as eager to make love as Colden was—more so, even—nights when he had to muffle her with a pillow because she was moaning too much. Sometimes she had to pretend to come so she could get her head up and breathe. Colden used to call their lovemaking "rearranging the furniture," because the bed or sofa or chair they were on had usually moved a couple of feet by the time they were finished with each other. But for weeks now, nothing. Leilah felt dead from the waist down.

Closing her eyes, she thought of Colden pinning her arms against the headboard, one on each side, crucifixion style. She thought of how he liked to kiss her breasts and draw lines on her belly with his tongue—swirls and circles that might have been branding symbols made up of Cs and Ls.

She slipped her left hand between two buttons of her

denim shirt, which had been Colden's before it shrank in the dryer, and began to rub her right nipple. She was trying to imagine what it would be like to actually use her breasts, to have an infant literally suck its life from them, when a loud thud above startled her. The boy upstairs was making the kitchen dishes rattle on their shelves again.

She stood and unbuttoned her blouse, unzipped her blue jeans, and ran a hot bubble bath that foamed with the scent of lilacs. She slid under the white layer that floated on the water like cream on milk. As the tiny bubbles popped, tingling her skin, she imagined thousands of tiny, manicured fingertips tapping her, lightly. She didn't touch herself until the water had grown tepid. The shiver was pleasant but not very strong.

The negligée she put on afterwards was navy polyester, but it felt like silk. The eyeliner was navy, too. She fluffed her shiny blonde hair and, looking in the mirror, became aroused again. Was she attracted to herself, she wondered? Then: could she be attracted to a woman? A thrill that felt both hot and cold, like the flash of danger she had felt stealing earrings that time when she was thirteen, ran through her body. As she lay down on the bed, she heard Colden's key in the door.

"Leilah?"

She turned her head on the pillow and saw the sun glint on Colden's glasses, a circle of light on each lens, as he walked down the hallway towards her.

"You seem starry-eyed," he said. A vapour of beer hung in the air between them as he spoke, which meant he had gone to the pub with Derek after the game. "What are you doing in bed in the middle of the day?" There was a cautious desire in his voice, but before Leilah could reply a sudden crash made them both look to the ceiling.

"Our kids won't behave that way, I know that!" Colden said, leaning over to kiss his wife.

Ever an ad man, Leilah thought. It's his second nature to try on ideas for size, as if they were new clothes.

Suddenly she decided to tell Colden the story of her morning. "I saw a man in a skirt on the subway."

Colden grabbed the clean black dress lying on the bed like a ghost and held it up to his waist. "Like this?" he asked, and then danced the can-can.

But instead of laughing, Leilah began to cry. Colden, frightened, dropped the dress and put his arms around her.

"What is it? What have I done?"

That was the worst of it, she knew: he had done nothing. They were a normal young couple, with the usual issues to sort out between them, the big decisions being less important than the day-to-day. But it was the day-to-day that she was worried about, because she had somehow, gradually, put her love for her husband into cold storage, and she wasn't at all sure she could get it out again. It scared her that she thought she could probably leave him, if it came to that; but whenever that day did or didn't come, she would probably be all right.

She would talk with Scott in the morning, and tell him about the man's red shoes, bobbing up and down on the subway, and she would ask him how he kept things going with Steven, and why. But for now, with Colden holding her, she could think of no way of explaining how much sorrow there was in a wife scrambling eggs in a kitchen.

Feliz Navidad

It was a Christmas of firsts: neither had ever been to Mexico; they had never vacationed as a couple; and, after a decade of holiday seasons with Julian, she would not be with him this year, or ever again. None of it felt right.

The flight was difficult to arrange on short notice, and the resort had no vacancy until the second day of the trip, so to tide them over she made a reservation for the first night at a place she didn't know. Their room there was small and dirty and forlorn; the water wasn't running when they arrived, at two in the morning, and the upright toilet lid had a cartoon sketched on it in black magic marker. It was of a mustached Mexican wearing a sombrero and pointing into the bowl with an oversized finger. The caption read, "Gringo, don't flush tissue paper—use the wastebasket!"

He took one look at the sheets pocked with cigarette burns and laid their coats across the bed. "Better off keeping our clothes on," he said, lying down with his back to her. She felt terrible for having brought him here, and was sure he would blame her for the miserable night they were about to put in.

They rested for a few hours and checked out as soon as they woke up. On the way to the resort, she made herself feel better about last night's mistake by composing, in her head, a letter she would write on her leftover Getaway Vacations stationery, when she got back home. She would berate the hotel manager for the shoddy conditions, and she might even threaten not to pay. Perhaps—

She was starting to think like her husband, she realized. She had always taken on the views of whomever she was involved with, but this was the first time she had heard herself *think* like him. The new voice pleased her a little, because she knew she must be making progress of some kind; but it saddened her, too, this glimpse of herself as someone so thoroughly separate from Julian.

She shook her head as if to knock his being out of her mind. He had left *her*. He'd gone to Brazil to do a workshop on urban farming, and he'd never come back. He sent a single postcard with a photograph of buildings so tall and close together that people on the sidewalks passed through long stretches of unbroken shadow in the middle of the day. On the back he'd written, "Sao Paulo in springtime. You see? I've much to do." His best friends, who ran an organic food operation at the Farmer's Market, received long letters that told another story. She knew this because they had finally shown them to her when she wouldn't stop coming to their stall, mooning about. They had to put her in a taxi and tell the driver where she lived, that day. She hadn't seen them since.

"Hola, honeymooners!" the vendor asked as they passed his beach stand, holding hands. The husband shook his head and said, "No, gracias" to the old man's brightly striped blankets. They were not to cart back tokens of the trip—that was the rule, because he hated the clutter of souvenirs and he didn't like to spend money needlessly. They were to use all of their pesos for food and consumable pleasures. Luckily, he said, since she was no longer on medication, she could indulge in margaritas and piña coladas and daiquiris all she liked. So far, she hadn't had a single sip of anything.

It *was* their honeymoon, in a way, though it had been six months since the wedding. He couldn't rearrange his shifts without at least three months' notice, so they had to wait until Christmas to go anywhere. He was an emergency physician who preferred, he said, the graveyard shifts, because he felt that what he did then mattered, and that great decisions had to be made in a moment. She hadn't slept well since they arrived because she was not used to his body lying next to hers at night.

By noon the sun was daring them to swim. They found sections of sand that were velvet to their feet, and they splashed and kicked in the foamy retreat of waves, still holding hands. Then he let go quite suddenly—almost threw her hand away from him—and dove into a gargantuan crest just before it crashed on shore. Some of the sunbathers, mostly pale, puffy, middle-aged couples bursting out of their swimsuits, shrieked their pleasure and ran towards the hotels that lined the beach. Others were caught before they had time to grab their coconut oil, magazines, transistor radios and towels. She stood fast, resisting the pull as the water dragged sand from under her, tickling her feet, grain by grain.

She watched her husband enjoying himself and thought, "What would I do if he were washed away?"—inciting herself to think the worst: lifeguards on sea-doos tearing out towards the horizon, then turning back again, slowly; crowds surrounding her with strange comfort, whispering that she must be in a state of shock, it was the only explanation. And perhaps she would be, but she suspected that she might feel exhilarated, too, and very free.

It hadn't been that way with Julian. She hadn't been that way. She almost died, after he left her, but the bottle of Tylenol 3 sent her no further than flashing lights and the white of the emergency room. The man who was now her husband had saved her. Saved her, and then courted and married her. He thought her pixie haircut and round brown eyes that stared and stared gave her an air of magic and innocence, both. For her part, she was simply too bewildered to resist any offer of love.

Her husband was walking towards her, but the sun was behind him and she couldn't see his face. She admired his lean body, his form silhouetted by the light that also made the water look like some precious liquid, like a body of melted, turbulent silver. When she realized that he could see her clearly, she waved and smiled.

"What do you want to do now?" he asked. He wrapped his arm around her, and cool water dripped on her waist. "Parasail?"

He was teasing—he would never expect her to be so adventuresome—but she had, in fact, thought about it earlier that morning. She imagined being pulled up off the ground, gliding far above the beach and floating over the ocean, and she imagined experiencing the exultation of absolute solitude and uncertainty.

What she said was, "It might be fun, but I can't help but think that the rope might break, and then I'd be lifted up and away ... from you."

"No one has had an accident so far. It must be safe, or they wouldn't let people do it."

"Why don't you try it, then?"

"You know I don't like heights," he said, annoyed at her for making him say it. His tone made her nervous, because his mood could shift so easily, and it pulled her along with it when it went in the wrong direction. He was right: she should have known. She knew him at least that well. At home his desk faced the door, not the window, because their condominium was on the fourteenth floor and he couldn't stand the view. He had bought it anyhow, because it was such a good deal, and he would be able to sell it in a couple of years for a large profit.

He took her hand lightly and they went back to their small cottage, where their breakfast things were still on the patio table. The mango she ordered every morning, scored and arching in its skin, was only half eaten. Her husband sat in a wicker rocking chair and closed his eyes. She did not want to sit still long enough to think. She wanted to walk, to find some other, errant rhythm that would break the silence between them.

"Let's go into town for lunch today," she suggested. She was playing with her wedding ring, which had his name engraved inside. "My treat!" He had given her the money she carried, so it was a little joke between them when she offered to pay.

They went in to dress. She put on her yellow skirt with the scalloped hem (he called her his Tulip when she wore it) and he wore his turquoise shorts with a clean white tennis shirt. He had carefully combed his hair into place after blowing it dry. It was one of the things she should like about him, this concern for his appearance. He had nicked himself shaving again and the tiny patch of tissue he had stuck to the cut was still on his cheek. He peeled it off at the same moment she reached her hand towards his face.

They left their cottage and walked by the frond-topped bar, the monkey cage and the hot tub in which a large European woman spent most of the day. Three or four Mexicans, members of the security staff, lounged about in the driveway. There were pistols in their belts. No one looked at the couple as they walked through the guilded gates.

She liked being behind the compound's walls and felt somewhat anxious venturing out into the city. Not far from the hotel, beggars were crouched along the roadside. Wrinkled, thin women of all ages, some with infants wrapped in colourful woven cloths, held their palms out meekly. He kept walking, but his wife slowed down, and kept looking back.

She remembered Julian's disgust with her travel agency's glossy brochures about places like the Dominican Republic and India, and she knew he would never hide himself away in an expensive resort if he were to go to Mexico. He was right to abandon me, she thought. She had to say in her head, over and over, "It's my honeymoon, it's my honeymoon," to keep herself from sinking.

"You can't help it that you're on vacation. You're just a tourist, remember!" He kissed her, his sensitive bride, on the brow.

It's my honeymoon, it's my honeymoon, it's my honeymoon.

They reached the outdoor market where hundreds of vendors were crammed behind counters and boxes, their tented booths separated by bright cotton dresses and hammocks and embroidered table coverings. The blankets, stacks of them, were exactly the same as those they'd been shown on the beach, only more expensive. A man shouted at them, "Here, signor, a nice necklace for the lady? A present for Christmas, si? Only one hundred pesos, for you!"

"A hundred! Sounds like a lot to me. I know that's dirt-cheap in Canadian dollars, but if you're used to Mexican prices you feel ripped off," her husband said to her. "What a con artist!"

She knew he would argue with the jeweller, even though he was not going to break his own rule to buy a trinket for her, so she distracted him. "Let's find some lunch before we're tempted by all this silver," she said, and they left to cross the bridge again. The temperature was eighty-five degrees and climbing, and the heat was close and wet.

He took her hand and rubbed her ring finger. "Looser?"

She nodded. She hadn't eaten very much for some time before the trip, and her clothes no longer fit as well as they had in the summer. The petals of her skirt hem grazed the concrete as they slowly walked along the sidewalk, Santa Claus piñatas hanging from clotheslines and telephone wires above their heads.

"I guess they have to beat their Santas to get any presents down here. How do the kids reach them?" he joked, but she didn't hear him. She was looking at a small boy huddled in the shade by the stairwell leading to a restaurant under the bridge.

The child had his eyes shut, and his head rested on his chest. A box of Chiclets was next to his curled-up legs. She found a ten-peso coin in her pocket and placed it in his outstretched little hand. His fingers curled around it, but he did not open his eyes. It wasn't exhaustion alone, she was sure, that had worn him out. His lips were a strange bluish-purple colour and his eyelids were crusted over. He was pale and thin, thinner than any other beggars they had passed that day. His legs looked like pencils that would snap if he stood on them. He was obviously a sick little boy.

Her husband tightened his grip on her hand and pulled her along down the steps and into the restaurant. He wouldn't let go until they were seated.

It was an open-air restaurant that smelled of garlic and chicken. He ordered two cervezas and looked at the menu. José Feliciano was singing "Feliz Navidad," and the record played over and over.

"Surely there are other songs you could play?" her husband asked the waiter, but apparently the only English he knew was on the menu. She let him order a chicken tortilla for her but when it came, she could not bring herself to eat it. He finished his meal and then hers, after she pushed her plate towards him. As he ate she stirred her iced tea with a coloured glass swizzle-stick that was shaped like a candy cane. After lunch, by unspoken agreement, they went back to the resort by a different route.

The next day at breakfast when she was still too quiet, her husband said, "Let's go find him. We'll shop at the grocer's by the bridge. We'll take some juice and oranges and a sandwich to him. It's the best we can do."

She was as surprised by this as if he had suddenly declared he would no longer be the person that he was. Of course, Julian would have come up with a plan just like it; Julian would have been as disturbed by it as she was, but he would have done something to help, and she would have expected him to. But her husband? Something shifted in her chest; she felt young and giddy and she laughed and held her husband's hands, both of them, in hers for what seemed a very long time, though it was brief. Then they walked to the bridge, but the boy was not there.

The return flight was a red-eye, so they left their hotel at midnight. When they got to the airport, none of the shops or cafeterias was open. They sat in the empty lounge to wait for boarding, and after a few minutes her husband dozed off. It seemed like it was the first time since they'd left home that he had not paid attention to her. She became agitated, and her legs tingled a little. She pretended there was sand underneath her feet that was gradually being pulled out to sea, and she held her shoes firmly on the floor until the feeling went away.

Other travellers began to arrive. She recognized some of the passengers they'd flown to Mexico with. At first she was alarmed by that coincidence, but then she remembered that it was a chartered plane, that of course they'd be leaving on the same flight, and that there was nothing more than that in it.

Her husband stirred. She leaned over and sang, "I wanna wish you a Merry Christmas," softly in his ear, and he opened his eyes. She smiled at him then, and decided that the trip had been a success.

When she lifted her hand to stroke his head, her wedding band slipped off her finger and slid through his hair. He held still as if he were trying not to anger a bee that might sting him, and when the ring bounced from his shoulder she clapped her hands and caught it between her palms.

The Halfhearted Winner

Carole turned off Bay Road and drove down the unpaved lane, looking for the red-barn-style mailbox she had been told to watch for. The ditches, she noticed, were strewn with old car parts, dismembered dolls, and single mittens and shoes. When she pulled into Joe's driveway, she saw a small handwritten sign on the front lawn that read:

"Furnit-

ure 4 U."

Pale blue paint on the small house was faded and peeling. Rust streaked from exposed nails in the shingle siding, and the roof sagged like the back of an aging workhorse. She didn't know how anyone could live in a place like this, and she couldn't imagine finding a piece of furniture inside that would be worth much.

She went to the back door, which was ajar, and stepped inside. In the dark, musty entryway, Carole bent to adjust the strap of her sandal, which had come loose. She didn't know that Joe had come into the room until she heard his smoker's rasp above her.

"Oh! You startled me, Joe," she said, standing up and straightening her skirt. "So. How are you?"

"Good, good. Nice to see you again, ma'am." She shook his outstretched hand, which was as rough as pumice. He always called her ma'am, which made her feel old (she was only thirty-seven) but also like a professional, like someone at quite a remove from dealers like himself who scoured flea markets and outdoor auctions in hardscrabble towns like Rockland, Canaan and Windsor Forks. They would turn items over in consignment antique shops in the city for a few dollars' profit. That was how Carole knew Joe: she saw him bringing a chaise longue into a store in Halifax, where she was shopping for a client, and she gave him her phone number in case he came across good quality items he could sell directly to her.

"I've been so busy that this is the first chance I've had to come see that table you called me about last week. Can I take a look?"

"Uh, afraid not, ma'am," he said, shifting his weight, not looking at her.

Carole scanned the room, searching the shadows behind Joe for the piece she had imagined would be set aside for her. "Where is it, Joe? Why can't I see it?"

"On account of I sold it last night. I was gonna call you later this morning—I sure didn't think you'd come out here so early. I feel real bad about it, but this fellow stopped in and saw it and offered me a lot of money if I'd let him have it right then and there, so I did."

It was going to be one of those days, thought Carole, a day filled with small disappointments, with little losses.

When she got home, she pressed the "Listen" button on the blinking answering machine. There was a message from her newest client, a canyon-voiced New Yorker named Rachel who had "absolutely fallen in love with Nova Scotia" during her summer vacation. She wanted several pieces of Loyalist pine furniture shipped to her home, which was just outside of Newark, and she wanted it as fast as Carole could find it for her.

"Hon, I'm still waiting to hear from you! Don't forget about me!"

"Rachel, I'm afraid that would be impossible," Carole said. The next voice on the tape was her friend Janine, reminding her about their lunch date the next day. Good, she thought. There's another afternoon filled. Grant's business trip would last at least to Friday and, while she enjoyed having the house to herself now and then, Carole didn't want to spend all week alone. The last message was from Grant. "Hey babe, *c'est moi*. I'm at the Calgary airport with time to kill, so thought I'd check in. Are you gonna pick up the phone? You're not still asleep, are you? Okay. Ciao for now."

She remembered a time when Grant's voice on the phone could make her blush. Listening to him was better than eating buttered lobster; she could almost taste his voice, it was so rich. Before they dated she would call him just to hear it, ordering items her company didn't really need. He'd been an office supplier's representative in those days; his sales visits led to lunches, then longer lunches and dinners, and eventually, they wed. That was ten years ago, thought Carole, as she erased the messages. Ten years! Sometimes she wondered how they had stayed together, and sometimes, why. But together they had stayed, and now, it seemed, they had finally reached some level ground.

She made some coffee and sat at the kitchen table, where she usually read the newspaper after Grant left for work, taking the Sports Section with him. She looked through the classifieds first, scanning the columns of Articles for Sale, Household Goods, Antiques, and sometimes even the Personals. There was so little creativity in the ads, which all sounded the same: SWM in his 50s seeking 25 to 30-year-old female for romantic interludes; widowed woman, still attractive, looking for companionship and friendship; bi-somethings available for discreet encounters. Janine, a travel agent, sometimes talked about placing an ad that would say, "Divorcée has free tickets to paradise for the right guy," but she was only kidding.

Under Auctions, an advertisement reminded Carole that the Lord Nelson Hotel was going to sell off the personal effects of Mrs. Neil Stafford, a wealthy Haligonian with a large estate, on Thursday. She skimmed the tiny type looking for pine. *A lovely lot, not to be missed! Just some of the items are fine bone china, some of the nicest jewellery we've seen, two slipper chairs, MacAskill prints, pineapple motif bedroom set, crystal vases, lamps, highboy, bevelled mirror in good condition, nice pine sideboard, and so much more we haven't room to describe! You have to see for yourself.*

"Amazing what old junk people will buy up," Grant had said—too loudly, Carole thought—the one time he attended such a sale with her. He had become a corporate real-estate agent, and he liked things new, clean and ready made. She tried not to feel slighted, telling herself he didn't mean anything against her career—or against her—but it had bothered her nonetheless, and that night she had gone on a cleaning frenzy.

"Relax, won't you?" Grant had said when she dusted the screen during an important play in the third period of "Hockey Night in Canada." "Can I not even enjoy some sports in peace, once in a while? You have to have control over every goddamn thing I do in this house—from when I can watch TV to when I can eat, to when . . ."

"What?"

"Oh, forget it," he said, but Carole knew what he was thinking: *to when we make love.* Not that there was much of *that* going on, not since the four miscarriages in her early thirties, and certainly not since the affair. They had gone months afterwards living like brother and sister, and then she was the one to make the first move, not him. They finally got back on track, and he didn't push it until she was ready. But he was right: Carole did think that there was a time and place for everything. Sometimes she thought that

that had been the trouble with their marriage all along: they were functioning on totally different schedules.

She found the scissors in the kitchen drawer and cut out the ad for Mrs. Stafford's estate. She put it on the freezer door at eye level, with a banana magnet to hold it in place. The thought of the auction made her feel hopeful, as if the week would be made of interesting possibilities.

After having a short nap, something she rarely did in the daytime (Grant's flight had left awfully early), she decided to get going with her day. First she wrote cheques to pay the phone and power bills, and then she balanced her bankbook (or tried to—she finally wrote off a nagging twenty-dollar discrepancy). Later, she dragged the clothes hamper from the bedroom to the washing machine at the end of the hall, then went to Grant's walk-in closet to check for delinquent shirts. The light bulb swung from its chain, and a little glinting on a shelf caught Carole's eye. She reached up and touched a tape-cassette case, half buried in the pile of Grant's briefs. She lifted it down and read what was handwritten on its spine: *With Love, from Linda.*

"Oh no," she said. She felt dizzy and her lungs hurt, as if she'd run up three flights of stairs. "No, not again, Grant!"

He must have packed quickly, she thought, and not noticed he'd exposed it. Or did he want her to find it? She walked back to the living room. She inserted the tape into the stereo. She pressed the play button, and she waited.

"Dear Grant," the voice began. "Some things can't be said face to face, at least for me. So listen, Grant—I want you to hear this. I want to tell you the story of my life. The story of the spiritual progression, so to speak, of Linda Jensen. Because you, Grant, are the reason I've grown. Oh, I know we've been seeing each other only a few weeks now, but I have visions for our future together—"

A few weeks now . . . ah, so this was an old recording! It was part of the past! She almost laughed, at first, but as she kept listening—compelled by the soft voice that, strangely, sounded very much like her own—her relief fell away and was replaced by an uneasy sense of imbalance, and then by the realization that her idea of the other woman, the identity that she had given her, had been completely mistaken.

"What do I envision for us?" Linda asked. "That together we will find grace, that we will share a love greater than us both. For me: that I will be able to love God in other people. God has never been so real, Grant, as He is for me now. You've helped me find my framework for the world, do you know that?"

She went on about Grant, and God, describing some spiritual architecture that Carole couldn't really follow, and didn't understand. Grant? And God? It made no sense, but Linda sounded so certain, so assured and at peace with the world she'd built around her, that Carole felt not humiliation, not jealousy that her husband had been involved with this girl—no, what Carole thought she was feeling, though she wasn't certain what it meant, was remorse.

When the voice stopped, nearly half an hour later, Carole sat in her chair, stunned.

It had been during an argument that Carole demanded to know if Grant was seeing someone else. When he nodded yes, it was as if an avalanche had come down on her. She questioned the truth of every memory and the reality of every moment she had spent as Grant's wife, and she was suffocating. She went on for days like that, for several weeks, until she decided she either had to leave him or look ahead, only ahead. And, eventually, the thought of Linda became like a pebble in Carole's shoe, sometimes rolling about and surprising her with a small, sharp pain, sometimes slipping to the side, for a while, and not hurting at all.

The tape had clicked off, but Carole stayed in her chair. She was thinking about the night he told her it was over. He broke off with Linda, he said, because he loved Carole best after all. He also said that his sales were way down, and that living a double life was killing his concentration.

She knew now that it was not because of guilt or love or even for the sake of his career that he'd ended it. It was because Linda was too intense, and because she needed him too much. In the year of life that had happened since, Carole had not suspected that, not at all.

She rubbed the arms of her chair with the palms of her hands, to calm herself. She looked at the fraying slipcover and realized she had never noticed the purple flecks in the fabric before. She had assumed it was a pure rich blue, all these years, but there they were: fine purple threads, right there in plain sight.

At an outdoor café, Carole and Janine sat sipping sangria. A dog in a car parked next to the restaurant patio was barking and making Carole feel agitated. It was a very hot and humid day. Janine's skin looked like it was made of pink clay, thought Carole; her face powder had turned into a pasty film. This made her suddenly self-conscious, so she dug up a compact from the bottom of her purse to check her own makeup. She tucked a loose bit of hair behind her ear and said, still looking in the mirror, "Remember last year, when Grant was seeing that girl, that Linda?"

"Of course I do," Janine said. "He had the nerve to use my agency to book his so-called business flights, for god's sake. No offence, Carole, but what a young thing like that would want with your Grant is beyond me."

"I knew she was young. Now I know she was religious, too."

"So?" Janine said. "And how do you know that, anyway?"

"Yesterday I found a confession she taped for Grant and I played it. But that's not the point."

"A confession? Of what?"

"Of her love for him, her need for him, I guess you could say. It's an old tape, nothing to worry about—though I don't know why he kept it. Maybe he just forgot. Anyhow, I can't stop thinking about her today."

"Don't relive it, Carole. Grant ended it, and that's that."

There was a pause in the dog's barking, and Carole hushed her voice. "But she sounds so fragile, and hopeful."

"I'm missing something here," Janine said. "So she was religious. So she was naïve. So what?"

"But I've been hating her all this time, and she was so taken in by him. My image of her was all wrong. Grant had her at his feet because she believed in him, almost like some deity, ridiculous as that might sound. And I sent her that letter when I found her note in his jacket pocket, remember? Telling her how wicked she was—"

"Wait a minute. You did her a favour, sending that letter.

Especially if she didn't know he was married, which she probably did not. Are you saying you feel sorry for her?"

"Well, yes. But for me, too."

"I'm glad to hear you say that."

"Because all this time I've thought, 'I won, I won.' But did I, really?"

The women were silent for a few moments. Janine was holding a piece of red onion suspended on her fork. Carole watched it dangle as droplets of salad dressing spattered the white linen cloth on the table, spreading like an oily amoeba.

The dog in the car was whimpering now. "Has anyone checked on that animal?" Carole asked the waitress as she walked by.

"We couldn't track down the owner, so our manager has called the police. It's such a crime. The windows have gotten all steamed up on the inside. Poor thing."

"It must be suffocating!" Carole stood up and crossed the patio to the gate. Janine called out to her, but she didn't turn back. She searched the ground for a brick or a rock, something heavy enough to break the car window. Then she saw a man approaching from across the street.

"Hi there," he said, smiling. "Hot enough for you?"

"Yes. I mean, I was just wondering what is going on here. With your dog, I mean."

"I had a few errands to do," he said, opening the door with his key.

"Okay, then. As long as you're back," Carole muttered.

"Hey boy, how ya doing?" The man reached in to pet his dog, and it licked his hand between panting. After they drove off Carole stood by the curb, hating herself for not having stood her ground and getting his name, for not having told him where irresponsibility, neglect and cruelty can lead; kicking herself for letting politeness get the best of her.

Linda's voice replayed in Carole's mind all afternoon and into the evening: that trusting, soothing voice that had scared Grant off, and that now had somehow seduced Carole into caring about her.

Carole's dreams that night were filled with images she had buried long ago, freshly unearthed and black as topsoil: Grant admitting he had been with someone else, someone younger; Carole, not quite hysterical but verging on babble, saying he was her husband, that he had broken his vows—that he was not supposed to shred her life like this, not now, not ever! Then Grant was rushing towards a car on a street Carole had never been on before. The car windows were fogged over, and Carole stood on the sidewalk watching as Grant fumbled at the door. When he opened it, after what seemed like hours of trying key after key, she saw a pale, blonde woman inside. The woman lifted her head from the seat where she lay waiting. "I knew you'd come," she whispered. It was Linda's voice, of course. "I prayed that you would."

When she arrived for the pre-auction viewing, the exhibition room was filled with people milling about, making choices, setting hearts and budgets on china sets and treadle sewing machines. Carole examined the pine sideboard. Not a classic, but it might just do for her American, she thought, running her hand across the oiled grain.

"Cast your eyes to the front of the bus!" the auctioneer called out. The event was about to begin, so the audience took their plastic seats. The second-hand dealers went to their usual spot and stood against the side wall. Carole saw Joe join the line-up there. She wondered if they would be opponents today, if he would have the nerve to bid for the one item he knew she needed.

Box lots and bookshelves, lamps and headboards, porcelain dolls and silver coins changed hands as Carole waited.

"Isn't this a dandy? A more beautiful silver teapot I've never seen, and I've seen quite a few, believe me. What'll ya give me for it? Let's say, oh, it doesn't matter, I'll start low," he coaxed. "Thirty dollars. Who will give me thirty dollars? Anyone?"

When the sideboard was finally carried into full view, Carole knew that this was the one. She sat up straight in her seat, wanting to be tall and seen. There had seemed to be little interest in the piece during the viewing, and Carole felt lucky. The thrill of the game was always the same. Letting her card talk for her, Carole could control the price of the object, taking it as high as necessary or stopping when someone else's desire for it became greater than her own.

Only once had she erred, and suffered the winner's curse. Last spring, just after Grant had come clean, she bid far too much on a Victorian fire screen when one other woman would not give up the fight. Though it was not in very good condition, and though she did not have a client in the market for it, the screen was a rare find. Many people had been interested, but one by one they stopped bidding as the price climbed past their spending limits. Her last rival looked as though she couldn't afford it, but she kept putting her card high in the air as if desperate to claim it—as if it had some mysterious personal meaning for her—and this only made Carole want it more. Now when she touches the worn needlepoint cover in its mahogany frame, she sees the other woman's disappointed face, and she hears Grant's voice promising to stay, and she wonders why people always want what they cannot have.

After just three flashes of her card, the sideboard was hers.

"Sold, to Number 138. Congratulations—you must be one happy lady!"

She smiled over at Joe, who nodded as if to say he was glad there were no hard feelings between them. Her sideboard was being carried off to the next room, where it would be kept until she was ready to leave.

After bidding Carole usually felt hungry and celebrated her win or grieved her loss in a favourite restaurant before going home. Today, though, she had no appetite, so she paid for the piece, arranged its delivery, and walked to the parkade around the corner.

In the car, she took a deep breath and made a mental note to phone Newark as soon as she got back to the house. But first, she decided, she would stop to pick up furniture stripper for the fire screen. She would spend the rest of the day restoring it, and then she could put it on consignment before Grant came back home. He had never liked it much, she thought, and he probably wouldn't even notice or care that it was gone—though she couldn't be sure, either way.

Madeleine

I.

The music coming from the house was so insistent, so young and loud, that Gloria was sure Peter could not be home. She waited at the door, and, in a lull between songs, noted that there was no barking going on. Could Maddy be deaf already? When Maddy was a puppy, years ago, she had been litter-trained like a cat and had never been outside the house.

Just as the music started again she rang the bell, holding her finger down on the day-glo button. She hadn't seen one of those since she left the suburbs. She rang and rang, and then the music stopped, and the door opened.

"Oh—hi." It was Stevie's voice. Stevie, her boy. But this boy had no hair.

"Stevie, what happened?"

"Oh. Chemo. You know," he said, touching his scalp, and looking at his feet. "Cancer." He raised his eyes back to his mother's face, her pretty, smooth face with the white skin of a baby. Her hair was glossy black, now, chin length, with bangs; she reminded him of an Egyptian queen, like those he'd seen painted on parchment at the Tutankhamen exhibit at the ROM last summer. Other than that, she looked exactly as he remembered her.

"Why didn't anyone tell me?"

"Dad didn't want me to say anything the times you phoned. He said it would just upset you."

He thought she must be waiting for him to say more, because she was grasping her neck with one hand, staring at him. "It's okay," he said. "I'm okay now." Then he started to sing "Happy birthday," but before he could say "to me," Gloria groaned and grabbed the door frame with her other hand. She buckled then, a slow collapse right down onto the cement stoop, her batik sarong splaying to expose a slender thigh with purplish splotches like faded birthmarks. (He did remember that about her: when he was four or five, she would not play with him or even let him hug her because, she said, she bruised worse than ripe fruit.)

The gift Gloria had brought with her had fallen. Stevie reached into the bag and lifted out an unwrapped box. It was a new portable tape player. He smiled at Gloria, who had opened her eyes. "Up you come," he said, but he didn't try to help her. Before he went back inside, he added, "You can stay, if you want. Dad's taken Madeleine to the groomer."

II.

The baby would not sleep. Not even for an hour at a stretch. Her husband could sleep through anything, but most nights Gloria was wakened seven times between midnight and six, when Peter's alarm went off and he sleepwalked to the shower. She would have to wait until he got home for her bath. She lay on top of the bedclothes, her exposed red nipples swollen and raw, too sore to be covered by the soft flannel flaps of the nursing gown.

"Look at me, Peter. Look what he's done to me," she said in that deep, dramatic voice he had fallen for about a year ago.

"You're his mother, for god's sake," he answered. He

was putting silver cufflinks, a graduation present from his parents, into one of his ten starched white shirts.

"You think you're so big, don't you? But you are a little, little man, Peter. You are not old enough to tell me who I am."

Peter was a bank manager now, though he'd been a teller when Gloria met him. She'd written a question on her withdrawal slip, smiling as she watched him read it, and when he looked up at her—he was blushing!—she knew that she had a date for the night. But he was nervous, passive, inexperienced, and their encounter was disappointing. After one particularly unsatisfying evening together, she thought he might be gay. She saw him a few more times when she had no other plans, but it was hardly worth the effort, from her point of view.

"The dry cleaner must just love you," Gloria said, watching him.

"I'm just a regular customer," he said, "and I have to look presentable to my clients. And I don't need your sarcasm, by the way."

Gloria stared out the window, watching as Peter's figure shrank to the size of a doll at the end of the long driveway. He got into the Buick and drove away from the dead-end street, leaving her alone with the baby for the day.

"I can't take this," she said out loud. Then, leaning over

Stevie's crib, seeing his miniature face pinched, red and wailing, she whispered, "I hate you!" The thrill of having uttered the three words made her want to say them over and over, louder each time: "I hate you! I . . . hate . . . YOU . . . !" Her voice seemed to still the baby into a startled state for a few seconds, but he soon began again. Gloria pulled the light blanket up over his head, then dropped to the carpet beside the crib. That was where Peter found her, hands over her ears, humming, when he came back home for his forgotten briefcase.

III.

When her mother telephoned, Gloria was taking a nap. She awoke to discover that Peter had invited her mother to visit, and that she'd arrive by train from northern Ontario the next day.

Gloria was wearing a terry bathrobe and slippers when she opened the door to greet her mother. It was three in the afternoon.

"What on earth?"

"Welcome to my world," Gloria said as she stumbled back to the bedroom. She did not come out when Peter came home, nor did she go to the table when dinner was ready.

Mrs. Prior fed Peter a solid supper of ground beef patties and canned peas. She bottled some of the powdered formula the drugstore had delivered for Stevie, and she put him on a feeding schedule that same night. Peter put his hand on his mother-in-law's shoulder and thanked her. "It hasn't been easy around here," he said, "as you might imagine."

"I raised her, Peter, but that doesn't mean I know her."

Mrs. Prior liked Peter, despite everything. He had wanted to do the right thing all along, but Gloria was not in love, not with him, and she resisted until it was too late to do anything else. The Priors had blamed the pregnancy first on the big city, then on the school system, and finally on Gloria herself, who had run away from home at seventeen to study at a fashion college and never gone back. When she called her parents to tell them about her problem, and to ask for money, her father hung up without saying anything.

"I don't know what we did wrong. Lord knows we did our best." Peter nodded. He was glad Mrs. Prior had come, but he had nothing to say to her. His own mother would never venture into an explanation or try on excuses for how he turned out—but then, she didn't have to. Peter had never done anything out of the ordinary, not one important thing in his life—except for getting mixed up with Gloria, and what was that?

The next day Gloria would not get up, no matter how long the baby cried or how often her mother demanded that she respond. When the curtains were thrown open, she moaned and put a pillow over her face.

"This is unnatural," her mother said. "You always were so theatrical, Gloria." She thought of the time the principal called her about Gloria's stash of aspirin. They'd found three bottles in her locker, and when she was asked to explain, she answered, "That's my escape hatch." Mr. Winters gave the matter some thought before calling her parents. When they met, he explained to the Priors that the class was reading *Romeo and Juliet* that semester.

"In all likelihood, there is nothing to worry about. That play has put many a young girl into a romantic fever." The Priors did not know what he meant, but they felt better after the appointment and shook hands with him before leaving. When Gloria joined the drama club later that year they were relieved, because they thought she would act out her moods on the stage and behave herself at home. But she didn't stay long enough for them to find out. And now look at her life: married, a nice husband, a house of her own … She would just have to get used to caring for someone other than herself, that was all there was to it.

"I'm your mother and you should listen to me. Because

now *you're* a mother. You have to take responsibility. This is the real thing, not some play you can back out of. Get up, Gloria. The baby needs his breakfast. Get up!"

"Just feed him," Gloria said. "Feed the little bastard."

IV.

Before Gloria left, she sat Stevie down at the kitchen table and pulled two pieces of bread out of the bottom of a limp plastic bag. She slathered them with peanut butter, and then, while he nibbled on the sandwich, she told her six-year-old son a story.

"The day you were born, your dad got smashed. I mean it—he got drunk and crashed the car into a tree. *That's* what he thought about being a father."

Stevie was kicking his feet against the legs of the chair. He stared straight ahead and seemed not to have heard what his mother had just said.

"He never was a drinker, so it probably didn't take much. The car cost hundreds to fix and so we couldn't even afford a new stroller for you. You had a second-hand crib, too. I think he's always felt guilty about that.

"The reason I'm telling you this is so that you realize I'm not the bad guy here. Or not the only one, anyway. I didn't know how to be a parent and neither did your dad. But the difference is," she said, exhaling and stubbing out her cigarette on Stevie's sandwich plate, "he's learning."

Still the staring, the kicking.

"Damn it, Stevie—don't you care if I walk out and don't come back again?" Part of her wanted him to cling to her knees, to demand emphatically with the whole of his small body that she learn how to mother him, though she was going to leave anyway. Part of her wanted to see him suffer.

Madeleine whimpered. Gloria knew that the dog, at least, would miss her. Peter had bought it when Stevie was one, as if Gloria hadn't enough to cope with. But as much as Peter doted on it, that dog was devoted to her. And all she did was put food in front of it, the dumb thing.

"Well, I guess I'm off." Gloria carried her suitcase down the driveway to the road. She had packed only one-fifth of her wardrobe so that she could manage the bag herself. She knew it would be pointless to ask Peter for any money, and what little she had she did not want to spend on a cab. She walked along the curb, not turning to see if Stevie was at the window, certain that he wasn't and that Madeleine was. She hummed "Que sera, sera" to cover up the poodle's yelps. Peter would go mad with the racket, she thought, smiling. She stopped to insert an unlit cigarette in the black lacquer holder she'd had since she was fourteen, put her sunglasses on, and kept going.

V.

Gloria had had a lot to drink. Quite a lot. She had been out with her boyfriend, a young company actor she'd met backstage at the Tarragon Theatre, where she worked as costume assistant. He told her he was moving to Vancouver right away.

"It's closing night," Tony said, "for *Fool for Love* and for us, too." He took her hand, and she shook it off right away.

They had made it through two bottles of wine by the time he said this, in his juvenile way. Oh, she had seen it coming. At her age, she couldn't expect anything more than an episode from a boy barely older than her son. But the fact of the matter was that she had hoped for more, or at least for more of the same.

When she got home Gloria washed her face and stared at herself in the bathroom mirror. The bulb was forty watts and she liked it that way. Very few lines—she'd always taken top care of her skin—and her fingertips found only the slightest puffiness when they lightly brushed over the area under her eyes. She looked into her pupils as she dropped her hands away, but a dark brown spot behind her index finger caught her attention in the mirror. Age spots, already? Gloria was thirty-nine years old. No one in her current life even knew that she was a mother.

She kicked off her shoes and made a gin-and-tonic at the kitchen counter. Tony would be on his way to Vancouver in the morning. He wouldn't likely be back for his T-shirts, books or black leather jacket. If he did come round, he wouldn't find anything, because after this drink Gloria was planning to gather what she could into a green garbage bag and toss it down the chute in the hall.

Another gin-and-tonic and she'd be over him, she thought. There were other actors to seduce. She was an attractive blonde yet, as long as the lighting was right. She was as slender as a teen and long-legged, and men still turned their heads on the TTC to have a better look when she wore her leather pants or a miniskirt.

The phone rang and she checked the call-display bar. The number was familiar but she wasn't sure whose it was. She said "Hello?" as if it were a real question.

"I tried you earlier but got the machine."

"Peter. It's you. Well, why didn't you just leave a message?"

"I couldn't. Not about this."

"Is it Stevie? A relapse?"

She'd made him promise to keep her in the picture, that day she fainted on his front porch, and—even though he didn't think she deserved to know—he'd kept it, more or less. She'd disliked the sound of Peter's voice more than ever, these past years, thinking he was calling with bad news the few times he did call. But it had been quite a while now since their last contact. Stevie had nearly made it to the five-year mark, when he'd be considered cured, or as good as.

"No, no. Not Stevie. Madeleine. I'm calling to say that Madeleine's dead."

For a moment Gloria felt both relief that Stevie was all right, and something of a suspended tenderness for Peter. She thought of the time she caught him bending down to pat Madeleine's head, whispering, "Good girl, good girl. Let's have breakfast now," as if she were human, as if the dog were his wife. That thought was what had made her laugh, and then the dog ran to her. Which made Gloria laugh harder, and Peter looked more miserable than she had ever seen him, except for the day after Stevie was born.

"I'm sorry, Peter," she said. "Poor old Maddy. Did she ever get over me?"

"She was my dog, Gloria. You left. You left her and me

and Stevie. None of us belong to you anymore. I'm only calling to tell you—"

As he kept on about the veterinarian's diagnosis and the pet crematorium, where a service would be held, Gloria thought of Tony pouring those miniature bottles of scotch into a plastic cup during his flight to B.C. Then she thought about the one time she'd been to Vancouver, on the sole family trip they took together, all of them, to visit Peter's parents. It was the first and last time they would meet Gloria, and their first sight of Stevie, who had just turned two. Peter refused to put the dog in a kennel, so Maddy made the trip also. Peter had made sure the travelling cage was large enough, but he worried for the entire flight that the luggage compartment was not sufficiently oxygenated. That was how he spoke; he said, "Stewardess, is the luggage compartment sufficiently oxygenated?"

Gloria accepted four or five gin-and-tonics from whatever trolley was gliding down the aisle. When they landed, Peter went to arrange for a rental car while Gloria stood at the luggage carousel, instructed to retrieve the cage as soon as it was in sight. Bags and boxes and strollers and suitcases began to flow onto the conveyor belt, and finally, the cage appeared. Gloria stood with Stevie on her hip, transfixed by the fact of Madeleine, moving.

The cage went around the circuit once, twice; when Peter came back it was on its third cycle, and Gloria was still watching. Peter thought she was ignoring the poodle, as a cruelty, but really she was wondering how to make her feet move, how to take a step to claim what was hers.

Now he was on the phone, telling her that the pet he cared so deeply for had died, and she wanted to tell him about that time at the airport so that he wouldn't think so badly of her. He was probably sitting in the kitchen, she thought, his tie loosened and his straight hair slightly separated into silver-peppered hanks, mourning a mutt that had never really returned his affection.

"Why haven't you remarried, Peter? You could have found a nice woman to share that big house with. Someone nicer than me. Wouldn't be hard to do, would it?" Gloria realized she must have had too much gin because she actually wanted to invite Peter over. "Peter, if you want to come here to talk—I mean, if it's not too late already ..."

"It *is* too late, Gloria. That's exactly what it is. I don't need anything from you. I'm calling just because, and for no other reason."

But he stayed on the line, saying nothing, and so did Gloria. She was waiting for Peter to hang up first, whenever he was ready to go.

Hugging Zero

Mary Beth stood at the stove, deaf to the rising shriek of the tea kettle. Dan stepped into the kitchen unnoticed; he ducked under the jamb, reached back to ease the screen door shut with his left hand. At the table he pulled his chair under him, the rubber-tipped legs bumping along the linoleum. Mary Beth snapped her head in his direction.

"Jesus Christ, Dan, I wish you wouldn't sneak up on me like that."

She took the last clean mug from the shelf over the sink. It had the Irving logo on it, from the days when she worked at a gas station in Halifax. Dan didn't know her then. They met after she moved back home, into her father's house, which needed some repairs even then. She had answered his ad in the *Masthead News*: "Dan's Your Man, If You Need a Helping Hand." He wanted to take care of her from first sight, but she didn't take help easily.

He watched her pour, fingers rattling a saucer on the teapot where the lid, lost or broken, should have been. Making do. She lost the vegetable peeler months back, too, and had to use a paring knife on potatoes, skinning them like apples. Dan liked to see her make spirals of the thick brown skin with holes where the eyes poked through. She must have boiled and mashed thousands of them to keep Steven, her father, alive all those months. Two days now since she'd been on her own.

"How ya doing?"

Didn't need to ask, could see for himself. Cigarette ends spilling over tuna can ashtrays on the table, on the counter, in the windowsill. Red eyes not from crying, but from a bottle. Tea was for remedy. Stringy hair, tucked behind her ears, needed washing. Still wearing the same stale jeans and wrinkled blouse from two days ago. Coffee splashed down the white front of the shirt like drops of muddy rain.

"That deer I got, it's almost ready to go. Another day or two and I can bring some meat over."

"Debbie went ahead and made the arrangements."

Talking to herself, as if he hadn't spoken. "Maybe I should have left him in his bed and burned the house down. Would've saved the trouble of cremating him, at least."

Dan sipped some tea, shuddered. Always a draught seeping into this house.

"I seen this TV show about people's last wishes," he said to get her attention. "This hunter hired some outfit in the States, can't remember the name ... well, it don't matter. Anyways, he had them mix his ashes with gunpowder when the time came. Know where he wanted to end up? Inside an animal's head, that's where. Actually got them to shoot the frigging cartridge into the skull of a bear. 'Cremains,' that was the company's name. Get it? Cremains?"

Mary Beth wasn't listening. She'd forgotten to puff on the burning stub that was almost down to the filtertip in her fingers, and was just staring through the torn sheet of window plastic they'd put up last winter. Handi-Wrap for houses, Dan had called it. He remembered running the hair dryer along the edge of the splintered window frame to seal it on. "Should keep you from getting freezer burn, anyways." Tried to pretend they were a normal couple, that Steven was not in the next room rotting away in his grimy pajamas, all he would wear for the duration, or that Mary Beth hadn't put off Dan's proposal a dozen times.

The deal was that the house would go to her. Mary Beth planned to sell the place for whatever she could get and maybe travel in the States once Steven died, but the kicker came when she wasn't mentioned in his will after all. He gave the house to her brother, Darren, instead. Darren, who'd left home at seventeen to study forestry at the University of New Brunswick and who had hardly come back except for his Christmas handout, something to get him through the next term at school. Darren, with a house of his own in Fredericton and a camp on the Miramichi—Darren got the house, not her. Mary Beth figured it was the only way weak old Steven had left to hurt her, and it worked. One last belt-whip from the grave.

Today she stood next to her sister Debbie in the chapel of Walker's Funeral Home. They'd been summoned by Reverend Percy, the minister for Lakeside Baptist. He was about Mary Beth's age, with lightly downed cheeks and steel-rimmed oval spectacles. From away—from Hamilton, or somewhere in Ontario, Mary Beth had heard.

"I know this is a difficult time for you, but I need your help. Because Steven never did come to church, did he? A bit of a wild horse, I hear. Anyway, I don't know a thing to say at the service tomorrow. Can you give me an anecdote? A memory of a good time you shared with your dad, perhaps?"

Debbie gave the question serious thought, avoiding Mary Beth's scoffing eyes. Debbie had tried to convince Mary Beth that she should forgive their father before it was too late, but instead Mary Beth had stopped speaking to her sister. They had been close once, grew up mothering each other and Darren, too; but then Debbie was converted by her born-again man, Eugene. Eugene was afraid of Mary Beth, who ignored more sins each day than he could possibly count, and he tried to get Debbie to stay clear of her.

"Hey, I know!" Mary Beth's voice broke the still chill of the room. Reverend Percy nodded, and Debbie smiled as Mary Beth began: "I got just the story for you. You see, there was this one day he was drunk, no more than usual, but this time he got his shotgun out. He lined us three kids up in the kitchen," she said, turning to her sister. "Remember?"

Debbie, although her smile stayed, shook her head to say "No" or "Stop," but Mary Beth paid no heed. "First he said 'I ain't your father,' to me." She held her arm straight out, aimed it at her sister, before continuing. "Then he said 'I ain't your father,' to you." Mary Beth glanced at the minister a second before her arm swung towards him. "He told Darren, 'Christ, maybe I am your father, but god only knows.' "

Debbie was sniffling as Reverend Percy, bowing his

head, walked away. Mary Beth was trembling, exhilarated, the best she'd felt for days.

She took the teabags out of the pot to poultice her eyes—Steven's trick—and lay down on the cot by the stove. Later, she woke because of a pounding that wasn't only in her head. Her neighbour, Jimmy Stokes, was knocking on the door.

"Let me in, goddammit!"

He pushed past her into the kitchen and she noticed two trickles of blood on the back of his balding head. Still sleepy, she let herself remember the maps they used to have pinned up at the gas station, with those thin red squiggles marking rivers ... or were they roads?

"Ellen whacked me with a frying pan!"

Mary Beth poured a rye for him and found a clean enough cloth under the sink. She ran water over it and gently wiped at the cut.

"A flesh wound, is all. Bet you'll bruise bad, though. What did you do to deserve this, anyway?"

"Nothing, that's just it. Drank my six-pack and had a snooze. Not a damned thing I don't do the same every night." Jimmy swallowed the last of his shot and held the glass out for more.

"I'll be clearing out of this place soon. Darren got the house but my guess is he's going to rent it out. I imagine you won't be able to run over here every time Ellen goes off her rocker, not after I'm gone."

"Ah, she'll calm down. Temper just needs to get vent now and then." Jimmy smiled, and the sight of his chipped and missing teeth made Mary Beth worry her own with her tongue. She was proud of them, still perfect but for the coffee and cigarette stains. One of the first things she did when she started working was to get regular check-ups, something she had let lapse for a while now.

Jimmy swallowed what was in his glass, put it on the table. "Hey, where will you go, an apartment in town again? Or maybe with Dan at his cabin?"

Mary Beth frowned at his foolish smile. "Don't you start in on me. I just put in two years less a day for a man, father or not, and now I'm free. Homeless, maybe, but free." She tore the cellophane off a pack of Player's Light and lit another cigarette.

"You know what that song says, don't you?" Jimmy asked. "'Freedom's just another word for nothin' left to lose.'" He sang so badly that Mary Beth nearly choked laughing.

After Jimmy left she drank more rye, thinking on marriage. Dan proposed to her like clockwork, but she had never considered saying yes. She had lots of reasons. For one, she didn't think she loved Dan, not like she should. For another, she was the restless type, just like her mother before her. Mary Beth used to watch her mother fix herself up on Saturday afternoons, getting ready for a night at the Legion. She'd curl her hair by wrapping it around orange-juice cans and even with them on her head, she was some pretty.

When the bottle was empty Mary Beth began to tidy up a little. She put away the box of Band-Aids that she'd lifted down for Jimmy's cut, though he wouldn't let her use one because he didn't want the adhesive to pull on his hair. Mary Beth remembered picking at a scab on her knee, the day after her mother left, thinking she would leave the grey, gummy outline of the Band-Aid's glue right there until her mother came home to wash it away. She woke up the next morning, and the next, and the next, with a hollow feeling worse than hunger in her belly. When she gave up hoping that her mother would walk in the door, she finally scrubbed at the blackened edge around the scar. That night she cooked her first supper for Darren and Debbie and Steven—fried bologna on buttered toast—and each day became just like the one before. The only difference was how drunk and nasty Steven got. Soon Mary

Beth dropped her childhood habit of rating each day on a scale of one to ten, because she had realized that even a three would be a rare if not impossible thing. Mostly she struggled to hang on to zero, hugging the round shape of it with arms numbed to the strain.

It was after dark when Dan pulled into the lane. The light was out in the kitchen, but the door had been left open so he crept in as quietly as he could.

Mary Beth was sleeping on the cot, her post these past few months. Saved her running down the stairs to the sickroom five times a night when Steven would call her or cough, or when she'd wake up because he hadn't done either in a while.

Dan crouched close, whispering at her thin face, "Mary Beth." He kissed her forehead. "Wake up. It's me."

She smelled like booze, like Steven, in fact. But she looked like her mother, he'd seen pictures. Dan wondered if Steven had ever tried anything, but was sure he'd been too tanked all the time to bother about that business. He'd lost his winter job long before he got sick, because of the drinking. Mary Beth told stories about Steven driving the village snowplow when he was sloshed out of his mind; in bad storms he would carve crazy paths down Bay Road and up private lanes in the snow, the sheriff following close behind with his light flashing orange all the way.

Moonlight oozed through the yellowed window-wrap, enough to see by. Dan washed the cups and plates that had been left on the counter for days, watched the bits of dried egg and breadcrumbs swirl down the drain while he worried about Mary Beth.

He wiped the back of his itchy hand against his chin. The sandpaper sound reminded him to shave for the funeral the next day.

Debbie and Eugene arrived with Darren, whose wife had stayed in Fredericton with the new baby. Three years since their wedding and Darren home once to visit. Mary Beth hardly recognized him, all clean-cut and wearing a good suit that you couldn't buy anywhere local. He'd become the manager of a mill, and he sure dressed for the part.

Debbie, who hadn't spoken to Mary Beth since her sister had pulled the stunt on Reverend Percy the day before, said, "Darren wants to speak to you alone." Eugene went with his wife to sit near the altar.

Darren cleared his throat. "So he's finally out of the picture, huh?"

Mary Beth took a cigarette and lighter from her purse and tried to get a flame, but only sparks shot from the flint.

After Darren handed her a book of matches, she said, "Things haven't turned out the way I planned."

"Dad called me a couple of weeks back," Darren said. Mary Beth blew smoke from the corner of her mouth, keeping an eye out for Dan, while Darren spoke.

"He knew you wouldn't be able to afford fixing the house and he asked me to cover the taxes and whatever work it needs. That's why he put the house in my name, so I'd be able to help out without an argument from you."

Mary Beth was confused, wary of a trick. She drew on the cigarette again, pinching her eyes half shut to keep the smoke out, and waited for her brother to go on.

"I'm not saying he was a saint or anything," Darren said, "but knowing he was dying did something to him. Made him realize what you'd done for him, if nothing else."

"I wouldn't have gone near him or the house if I hadn't lost my job, and you know it."

"Point is you did. That house is yours. I'll put it in writing if you like."

Reverend Percy had started the service so Mary Beth dropped the cigarette onto the tile and ground it flat with the toe of her shoe. She said nothing to Darren as they walked into the chapel and sat at the back of the nearly empty pews. Jerry was up front, the bruises on his scalp green as grass.

"Courage is needed at times like these, facing the death of a family member," the minister was saying. "But if we endured no hardship, how could we appreciate better days? You see, we have to count our blessings. Sometimes we have to look for a blessing to count, mind you, but that is what the Lord teaches us to do."

Dan slid in next to Mary Beth, touched her knee. His fingers covered the dried drop of red nail polish she had used to stop a run in her black nylon.

"Let us remember Psalm 90, where Moses tries to understand man's mortality. Verse 9 reads, 'We spend our years as a tale that is told.' And he's right: life, like a story, has a beginning, a middle, and—sad as it may be—an ending. But life needs this shape to have any meaning. And so, knowing this, Moses eventually begs God to 'Teach us to number our days, that we may apply our hearts unto wisdom.' Children, mourn not for Steven, whose story has ended. Remember, it is because our days are numbered that life is so precious."

"I'll mourn not, all right," muttered Mary Beth at the same time that Debbie's wailing began.

Afterwards it was Darren who took Mary Beth home because Dan had to finish butchering his deer, he said. Mary Beth knew he was just letting her have time with her brother. In her kitchen, she sat down and let her scuffed black pumps drop to the floor. Darren glanced at the room as if it were a movie set.

"My god, it's strange to be back here, without him in the house."

Mary Beth, annoyed, noticed a spasm start up in her brother's right eye, a nervous tic she thought he'd outgrown. He was looking out the window now, picking at a cellophane flap as if it were a hangnail.

"Debbie's over the top, isn't she? Eugene had to just about pry her off the coffin, for god's sake."

Mary Beth didn't respond. Debbie's behaviour was nothing new to her. If it surprised Darren, that was his problem.

He tried again. "I guess you'll want to sell up, once it's in decent shape."

"Decency's hoping for a lot." She softened her voice a little, remembering what he'd told her at the church. "Best we'll be able to do is make it a little more winter-proof. And Dan won't mind giving me a hand with painting."

"Dan would do just about anything for you, from where I sit."

"Well, I don't want to take advantage of nobody."

Mary Beth went for a walk by herself the next night

while Dan loaded venison into her deep freeze. At the end of the path that led into the woods, she turned to light a cigarette, cupping her hand around the flame to keep it from the wind. She looked up as she inhaled and saw a fuzzy outline, the smear of Dan's back, through the kitchen window. He was probably thinking that she would marry him, now that Steven was gone. But really, she hadn't decided what she would do next. All she knew was that her days with Dan were numbered, and—even if some of those days might rate a four, five, or possibly a six along the way—she knew that she would eventually leave. Eventually. She would.

She found herself crying for the first time since Steven had died, though not for him: she cried for all that he was not, and never had been; and for all that she was not, and never would be; and for the despair of Dan's desire for her, which she could do nothing about. She stood a good long time in the crisp fall air, thinking and crying.

Mary Beth cut her walk short and headed back towards the house. Knock it off, she scolded herself, because she didn't want to give Dan the wrong idea, to make him think she wanted comforting. But he had heard her rustling the leaves in the yard and was already waiting at the door when she got there. He held it open for her, and she went in.

Strange Relations

I. Stone Haven

We called her Daisy, and always had; she demanded that. She refused to answer to any name that resembled "grandmother." So Daisy it was, though as far as I could tell there had never been anything bright or fresh about her. She and my grandfather, Grim, were as mismatched as they were misnamed. My older sister Gwen, when she was learning to talk, had trouble pronouncing "Grandpa"; her word for him was Grimpa, and when the rest of us, myself and the cousins, came along, we said it that way, too. So it stuck—sometimes as Grimpy, or Grimpapa, but mostly as Grim.

Grim had been dead for two years when the farmhouse in which he and Daisy had lived their entire married life was finally sold. Daisy moved to a small apartment in town, after which family reunions at Christmas alternated between our house and my aunt's. The first year, at Aunt Sue's place out by the airport, Daisy, perched at the head of the table, said, "I never wanted that house or the kids that went with it, you know. It was Bill. Bill wanted a family. Bill had to have his way, right from the start." She pinched her mouth shut between sentences. With her short white hair, peering through her black horn-rimmed glasses, she reminded me of an eagle, her round grey eyes shiny with excitement. "One wasn't enough, either," she added, staring at her daughter, who was pouring more wine for herself.

Sue, wearing a Santa Claus hat and a fuzzy red sweater, had a very pink face, as I recall—though it was probably because she had been drinking eggnog since noon, and not from embarrassment. We were all used to Daisy's outbursts, but her resentment of the lives she'd put on earth was especially strong that night. It seemed a physical presence, something hard and blunt and heavy. I admired my aunt, when she put the wine bottle down and said to her mother, "You maternal thing, you. Maybe it's not too late to give me up for adoption. How about it, Newman? Will you and Jenny take me in?"

Aunt Sue had put her crocheted tablecloth out for the

holiday meal. It had been her wedding gift from Daisy. ("What a miracle she didn't repossess it after your divorce," Mum whispered to Sue, who winked and said, "She tried. But I told her I'd just keep it for the next time around, to save her the postage!") I wasn't to meet Pierce for years, but I knew my own gift would be identical, because when Gwen and I were still children, Daisy had made the same rectangle of knots for both of us. (My male cousins, all three of them, would be given lawnmowers.) I doubted that Gwen, who had been wandering the country since she turned twenty earlier that year, would ever be back for hers.

I was twenty-four by the time my parcel arrived, wrapped in tissue paper and twine, in the mail. I read the note to Pierce, who by then had been living with me for three years (Daisy still called him "Mr. What's-his-name"): "May as well have it, looks like I won't live till you're wed. Daisy." I used it a lot when we were together, because it made our cheap press-wood table look sophisticated, but after our divorce I put it into storage. Each thread of it seemed like one of those strings you tie around a finger to remind you of an unpleasant task.

The summer I turned twelve Daisy and Grim sent me five dollars inside a card, as they did each year. Grim had written an extra line that said, "Have fun, Skipper." He'd started using the nickname because I was steered in the right direction, he said, and when he called me that, I felt that I was.

My father was surprised when I told him I wanted to spend some time at the farm, but there was nothing for me at home, with his relentless need for peace and quiet and with Gwen's tantrums. My sister was a door slammer, a yeller, a contriver of fits; she was also dangerous. Once, when I was four, she slid in behind and shoved me out of a chair, and I broke my leg. My limbs were always covered in bruises from pinches, punches and kicks. Other than in rage or deprecation, she rarely spoke to me. But she could be fun, too, and she had that ability to charm that some bullies use to hold a crowd. I envied her friends when I heard them laughing together.

Though three years older, Gwen was smaller than me. I knew she was angry that the treatments—for Hodgkins, for nearly a year—had left her with a child's body at a time when I was showing the bumpy beginnings of breasts. Maybe she was angry that she had survived at all, or so I would wonder later. My father explained her temperament, to himself at least, by blaming it on genetics, on Daisy; and my mother—well, she was detached from most of what went on when we were growing up. That pulling back, that ebbing and depletion ... Gwen would have felt the difference, whereas to me, for a long while, it was just our mother's way.

On the day that I decided I should go to the farm, Dad was in his den, the pipe that he puffed on occasionally hanging out of a corner of his mouth, and a thick novel on his lap. I stood next to him, breathed in the sweet tobacco aroma for a few seconds, and said, "I'm bored." I don't know what I thought he'd do; I certainly didn't think he'd jump up and say, "Hey, let's go to a movie!" or "Let's play catch!" as I suspected other fathers might. Perhaps I hoped only that he would notice me, which, in a way, he did: when I repeated myself, he took the pipe out of his mouth, pointed it at me, and said, very deliberately, "You can see that I am trying to read, Clara. It is not *my* job to entertain you."

So that afternoon I told my mother I wanted to visit Grim. She called Daisy, who was, apparently, delighted to hear of my plan, or so Mum said. She took from her closet an old Samsonite carry-on bag, but when I began to put my T-shirts and shorts and panties inside, she insisted on taking them out again.

"You know how Daisy is," she said. I did, and I knew how my mother was, too. The laundry usually piled up for three weeks or so, and Gwen and I were used to digging through the hamper to find a favourite shirt or jeans to wear just one more time. If my sister tried to do a load herself and Mum saw her putting a few things in the machine, she would sigh and say, "All right, all right, I get the message," and take over the task.

"Nothing is ever good enough for your grandmother. I won't have her seeing you show up without clean clothes. But don't be surprised if she insists on re-washing them. By *hand*."

The next morning my father took me to the bus station before he went to make rounds at the hospital. The town was only an hour away from Toronto, but to me it was a different world entirely. Along the way I saw, nailed to electrical poles, homemade signs advertising jams and vegetables and baked goods. We passed stretches of irrigated farmland I'd not noticed on the drives at Christmas, when the snow covered it like a crunchy meringue. Huge machines chugged through the dirt, tilling, I supposed, for the next cycle of seeds to be put in. Other fields were covered with leafy green growth, not lettuce, but not a vegetable I recognized, either. The houses, set far back from the road, were mostly painted white and seemed plain and modest compared to the suburbs, where homes like ours were lined up in rows, every third one identical to the first. I imagined these places to be well-loved, enduring, like the people who lived in them.

As the bus left the highway I saw another message, this one painted on the rock-face that ran alongside the off-ramp. It read, "Jason loves Robin," and a heart was drawn around the words. I wondered who would write something like that, out in the open; no one at our school would be seen talking to the person he or she was "going around with." Yet this declaration was made in bold red paint on a public road. Gwen's friends would roll their eyes and think Robin mortified. But Robin, I thought, might live in one of those white houses and Jason might work the farm next door to hers. I began to think of them as contented country kids who would be engaged before graduation and no one would think there was anything wrong with that. I began to fantasize that I could live with Daisy and Grim, and go to school here, too—I could become Robin's best friend! I'd help her pick out her wedding dress and plan her reception at the community centre or gym, and Jason's brother would be the best man and my date, and—

The bus pulled into the station, and when the driver turned off the engine it made a snorting noise before choking into silence. I looked out the window and saw Grim standing next to his old Ford. He had a straw hat pulled over his eyes and his hands were in his pockets. I climbed down the steps of the bus and ran through the parking lot towards him. "Hel-lo Skipper!" he said, bending down to hug me. "How was school this year? Learn your ABCs?"

"A long time ago," I said, laughing. His shirt was smoky, but I liked the scents of garden soil and wood shavings that were also there. He put me down, picked up my bag, and we got into the car.

On the way to the farm, driving over the dusty road that would be oiled into a brown stench at sundown, Grim pointed to a small wooden building. "That's where I went to school for a couple of years," he said. I knew he had had to stop going when he was ten, to help his parents run their farm.

"We didn't have paper, most of the time. So our teacher took us outside on dry days to teach us the alphabet. She wrote the letters with wooden sticks in the dust on the street." I could tell that this memory made him happy, and he whistled as we drove the rest of the way.

After the bus ride I had thought that the grass at Daisy and Grim's would be plush and moist, that the tomato plants would be plumping and that pansies would spill from window boxes, that ivy growing on the grey stone of the house would strive skyward. Instead the dry grass was yellowed, prickly to the touch and, I guessed, unbearable to tender city-feet like mine. Most of the garden would be harvested later, but now it was puny and the rows, ruchings of dry earth, sported spindly vegetation. Daisy didn't especially like flowers, not even her namesakes that were growing wild in the field beyond the garden, so she hadn't planted anything that would bloom.

When we walked into the kitchen, Daisy was pouring a pail of dirty water down the sink and the freshly scrubbed floor was gleaming.

"Well, missy," she said, squeezing my shoulder with her free hand, "what do you have to say for yourself?"

"Not much," I said. I wanted to cuddle Kitty, the old cat, but Daisy had other ideas. She put me to work shucking corn, the first of the season and very pale. Even I knew that it would be tough and tasteless, but Daisy couldn't stand to waste anything, so I went to the back porch to do what I had been told. I sat on an old lawn chair that pinched my thin thighs between the strips of webbing, making me jump (I thought I'd been stung and was glad Daisy was not there to see me flinch). I peeled the green leaves back and was surprised when the starchy smell of the yellow silk made my mouth water so suddenly that my tongue hurt.

After dinner, we played "Go Fish," the only card game I knew. Daisy had put a dish of peanuts on the table and poured a glass of ginger ale for each of us. She was in a very good mood, I thought. I could see myself staying for a few weeks.

"How about going fishing for real tomorrow?" Grim asked, after a few hands.

"Sure," I said. I'd never killed anything before, other than houseflies and some ants in the kitchen once. But fishing wasn't killing, not really. Grim did it. "That'd be great!"

"Now you're talking," said Daisy. "We can take a picnic lunch and show Clara how we country folk do things."

I came downstairs early the next morning without Daisy seeing me, and I watched her pack our lunch. She hummed as she wrapped chunky squares of cheddar cheese, watermelon, and egg-salad sandwiches in waxed paper, and then she started singing, her voice trilling and soft, a song that started with "Oh what a beautiful morning, oh what a beautiful day!" Then she stopped, and without turning around she called out, "Get down here, missy. Big day ahead!"

We drove out beyond the farmlands, parked on a side road, and walked between fields along a long line of trees—poplars, weeping willows, birch; Daisy named them off as we passed—until we reached a large pond with tall grasses and stones piled up around it.

"Donny Dimock made this fishing hole himself," Grim

said, squinting as he tilted his face up to the sun. "Put in a few trout and they just kept multiplying, like in the Bible."

Grim set me up with a rod and sat down next to me. We stayed like that for a few minutes without talking.

"Lazy as ever," Daisy said, looking at Grim. "You're not doing too well either, Clara." Daisy had already caught three good-size trout. When she pulled them in, she yanked each one free of the hook, and slid them through a square hole in the slanted flat lid of her straw fish-basket. Each one flapped in there for longer than I thought they could, and then they were still.

Grim had already baited my hook four times. Each throw of the line brought back weeds, for which I was grateful. I did not want to catch anything.

"Five times lucky," Grim said, winking as he handed the rod back to me.

I threw my line into the water again and watched small ripples, the kind skipped stones make, spread across the surface. Then I felt a tug.

"Reel her in, Skipper!"

I did have a fish, but it didn't resist at all. When I pulled it out, it was already dead. I'd hooked him in the eye, through the brain.

"Throw it back in! Please!" I said.

He did, and I hoped it would swim away, but it floated. Grim put his arm around my shoulders.

"Don't humour her, Bill. And you. What kind of a sport are you anyway, Clara? Don't be so stupid."

The hurt was instantaneous, furious. But when I looked at Grim, he was shaking his head just a little and telling me, without speaking, to forget about it, that it wasn't true and we both knew it. He calmed me with just that. Daisy was already packing up the lunch, uneaten, and heading for the car. "No point in staying here with no one wanting to fish. I don't know why I bothered."

Back at the farm, Grim took my hand and we walked over to the small barn with its painted sign over the door that said "Stone Haven." There hadn't been any animals in it for decades, and there were only a few chickens around, Dad had told me, when he was growing up. Now Grim used it for a woodworking shed and a smoking hut.

We ate some watermelon that Grim had taken out of the cooler when Daisy wasn't looking. He was the only person I've ever known who liked the taste of salted fruit. I shook a few grains from a yellowed plastic container onto my triangle and timidly bit into the cool, pink flesh. I loved it, the surprise of the sweet tang. I smiled at Grim and ate another piece, spitting seeds to the gravel floor as he had shown me to do. "Seeds belong on the ground, I'd say." I wanted him to be my father right then.

When it was all gone and we'd wiped our hands on our shirts, Grim moved a little way off to have a cigarette. I reached behind some lumber to take out a book I'd left there the day before, and opened it up. Grim looked over.

"What you got there?"

"It's called *Emily Climbs*. It's about a young girl who knows things."

"Like you, eh Skipper?" He smiled and gently brushed the hair out of my eyes. "Your dad liked to read when he was your age. I'd send him out here to feed the chickens and when I'd check to see what was taking him so long, I'd find him sitting over in that corner, reading something from the library."

"Did he like the chickens?" I asked.

"Oh yeah, he did. We kept 'em for the eggs, not for eating, and your dad named some of them like they was pets. But he should have paid more attention to them."

"What do you mean?"

"Well, one time he got into his book first and forgot to feed the chickens at all, and when his ma called him in to bed he forgot to close the door. The neighbour's German Shepherd got in and killed a few before I could get out there to chase him off. You can't have livestock and not keep them alive, that's rule number one. Your Dad had to learn it the hard way.

"Now. Go find yourself some shade and enjoy your story, while I have another smoke in here."

I walked towards the house but stopped at the well and pumped the black handle to fill a tin cup they kept there. But I miscalculated and a lot of water gushed over the rim, the force of it splashing my T-shirt and shorts. I had the feeling that Daisy would be annoyed with me for that, so I sat there in the sun until I dried off.

By the kitchen door, Kitty was asleep on a chair, his leash tied to one rung so he wouldn't spread black hair all over the gold crushed-velvet furniture in the living room. I petted him from head to tail, as Grim had shown me. ("Never rub the fur the wrong way, Skipper. That don't feel good to a cat.")

Daisy was peeling vegetables. There was a mound of brown potatoes in one pile and the peeled ones, white, in another, with something of both colours lying like strips of skin between them on the newspaper covering the kitchen table. Her hands were stained with mud and her knuckles were swollen and red and misshapen. I was going to ask if they hurt much, but Daisy spoke out first.

"What are *you* doing inside?" She hadn't forgiven my reaction at the pond. "Get yourself out in the fresh air."

"But Daisy, I want to read, and the barn is hot and the sun's too bright." I stepped on the white squares of the black-and-white checkerboard tiles of the floor, playing hopscotch.

"You've come in to *read*? Really, if that's not the icing that broke the camel's back!"

I laughed at the mixed-up expression, but Daisy hadn't meant to be funny.

"Who are you to come in here and back-talk to me, you little smarty pants?"

"I'm sorry—"

"Don't you sorry me, and don't you cry again, either. Clara Morrow, full of sorrow. Well, I'll tell you a thing or two, missy. Your father never got away with that kind of behaviour in this house, believe you me. Now go on. Get to your room, before I smack you for being such a royal pain in the you know what!"

I scrambled up the stairs and into the guest bedroom, where I had slept the night before. It had been Aunt Sue's room when she was growing up, and I guessed that she had spent many hours up there being punished for her own back-talking. I was upset, not only from the scolding but also because I had let myself feel so happy beforehand, out in the barn with Grim.

Later he came in with a tray of peanut-butter sandwiches and milk. I looked up from my book and smiled. He didn't say a word, but winked as he closed the door behind him.

Later Daisy called me down for supper. She'd fried the trout, and left the heads on. Grim watched me stare at the eyes, and then he reached over and took my plate to the counter with a knife in his hand. When he brought it back the head was gone, and the tail, too.

"Watch for the bones," was the only thing Daisy had to say.

That night when I went to the bureau in my room to see where Daisy had put my pajamas, I saw that one of the handles was loose, so I pulled on the other one until the drawer gave enough for me to ease it out with my hand underneath. It was empty, except for a slim pile of papers. I turned on the lamp and saw "The Life of Andrew Masters" typed on the first page. I knew from doing a family tree project for school that this was my great-grandfather's name. The second page said, "My tongue is the pen of a ready writer: Psalm 45." This line was written in an unfamiliar backwards-sloping steady hand that must have been his. The rest of the pages were typed but did not seem to be connected to each other, or complete.

I lifted the loose sheets of onionskin that crinkled like Daisy's waxed paper and put them on top of the bedclothes, after I'd crawled underneath. I sifted through the few sheets, mostly a record of the days Andrew spent "dry," as he put it, with a few anecdotes mixed in.

> *After the Larch wedding Jim and I were helping the bride's father home and the whole town watched from their verandas. Father heard from a family noted for their long tongues that we three were all the worse for liquor and, though I denied the story, having been off of it for two months, he said he had it from respectable members of town that they had seen me drunk. He said he was going to garnishee the wages he paid me at the store to prevent me spending them on drink. I left home and didn't speak to him again for the rest of his living days.*

I took the "long tongues" literally and laughed when I read it. I wondered if Daisy had copied out only the parts of her father's record that she wanted to keep, or if her arthritis had made her stop typing before she finished.

The next page told a ghost story:

> *When my good wife, apparently having been dead for some minutes, the pulse and breathing having ceased entirely and the hands and feet being icy cold, revived again, I cried out, "Lily, you're not dead!" and she said, "Not before you promise to keep off the liquor and keep up the house, so Daisy will have a home as long as she lives." So I said, "I will raise the toddler, don't you worry." Then she died again.*

It was getting late and I worried that Daisy might open the door to see why my light was still on, so I tucked the pages back where I'd found them and closed the drawer with as little noise as possible. The loose handle rattled some, so I left the drawer resting unevenly on its wooden rails and got back into bed and slept.

At the breakfast table the next morning, looking at my watch and waiting for a chance to phone my father to come and get me, Daisy said, "A kettle of fish never boils, Clara." I didn't laugh, but looked out the window to the barn, where I knew Grim was having his first cigarette and pleasure of the day.

Three years later Grim was in the Princess Margaret Hospital, where I visited him every day after school. He was being given radiation for lung cancer. My visits helped him keep his spirits up, he said. Dad dropped by occasionally on his way home from the general hospital where he worked downtown, and Aunt Sue and her kids came by every so often, too, but I rarely saw Daisy there. She came in from the farm on weekends, if a neighbour offered to give her a ride.

Once I asked Grim if he wanted his hair trimmed, because I knew it was something Daisy usually did, to save the cost of a barber.

"Now that's a good idea, Skipper." He sounded as though I'd offered him a cigarette, which he would have loved more than life itself.

The scissors I brought with me the next day from Mum's kitchen drawer weren't very sharp, but if they pulled at his scalp Grim didn't mention it. I held one silver-grey, silky section at a time, and cut half an inch off each. Brushing the strands back in place afterwards, I saw that the hair near his forehead was tinged yellow like corn silk. Some of the stubby dead ends stuck to my dampened hands, and when I went to wash them off in the tiny bathroom he shared with three other patients, I saw that they weren't silver or grey at all—they were really just bits of black and white.

After many visits Grim stopped calling me Skipper, and then, when he wasn't able to recognize me at all, he called me Miss. He didn't know Daisy, either, by then. And Daisy, it seemed, was anxious to forget him. She called the house one April evening and sickened me with her news. The mature telephone manner I was trying on had fooled her into thinking she was speaking to my mother, although it probably didn't matter to her who had answered the phone.

"I've arranged it all. He's not going to last long, so Sue and I have picked out the coffin and such. Just so you know things are taken care of."

It was horrible, what she said. But Daisy was right. He didn't last long.

The day of the funeral was bright. As we left the tiny country church I looked across the fields that were green with winter wheat. Soon the last of the snow would be gone, and that seemed about right. I remembered one of the last knowing things Grim had said to me: "Well Skipper, almost fishing time again. I sure will be glad to see the sun."

Daisy travelled a little after selling the farm; she took a bus tour around England and a couple of others through the United States. In her very old age, she didn't leave her apartment. That was when she started to write letters: the odd one to Gwen, whom we had tracked down eventually in British Columbia, and more frequent, longer ones to me, once I had married and moved to Saskatoon with Pierce. Typing had become too painful for Daisy, so she hand-wrote each one.

> *I hope you can make out my scribble, it sure is forbidable. My hands are not so good these days. Better to have arthritis than the alternative (dead, I mean). I sure do look back Clara to when you were little and the times I spent with you. I came to Toronto to see you in a play in kindergarden. The teacher was so surprised that I'd do that. But I was and still am your proud Grandma. Tomorrow is July 1st and we are promised rain again.*

But the relations Daisy had now given herself, the family she had taken on, finally, as her own, did not change her in the eyes of any of us. Though with me, I admit, she came close.

Dear Clarabell,

My mother was named Lily as you know and my father called her Lilybell because he thought she was so pretty, with her blond hair and blue eyes and all. You look a little like her, and so Clarabell it is. It was too bad that time when Grim and me took you fishing that you got homesick and had to leave so soon.

Daisy was a bright woman, I'd come to realize, sharp in more ways than one. Yet I usually responded to her letters with brief notes that would be of little interest to her. And I would wait a good few weeks before sending them, for fear of setting up a stubborn exchange I did not want. I'd answer her questions but would not ask any of her, nor volunteer information about my life.

During our marriage Pierce thought I was cold to keep myself so distant from the old woman, who was, after all, my grandmother. And he was partly right, but he'd met her only once, at our wedding, to which I hadn't invited her—Mum did that.

Later on my mother, of course, would have filled her in about our separation, but I never dealt directly with Daisy on the subject. I did receive a note from her not long after

I signed the divorce papers: "Secrets can kill you, Clara." The envelope also contained a faded, torn newspaper clipping, which I still have. There is a picture of Daisy and Grim—were they ever that young?—but Daisy is blurred, as if something inside her had vibrated and shaken the light. Underneath, in small, black type, it reads:

> *On June 4, 1928, Mr. William Morrow and Miss Daisy Masters were married by Minister P. Jameson. No family members were present.*

Though I'd never heard the date of my grandparents' marriage, the year meant something to me. My father was born in 1928. Two months after the wedding.

She never referred to the clipping again. And since, by then, communication had become infrequent between my parents and me, I did not have much of a chance to ask my father about it, even if I'd wanted to. I'm still not sure if he knows, but I would guess that he does, on some level. He had been a curious child; even Daisy said so.

I hardly knew her, but now I think Daisy was kind of like an onion. Cutting into the nugget of its core is bound to make you cry, but there is some sweetness, too, in an onion's sour heart.

Her letters kept coming for a while, but they became shorter and shorter, and less frequent. Up to the last, she twice underlined "I love my family!" at the bottom with a fierceness that almost made me believe her.

II. Visiting Hours

The first thing my father said to me, after finding her on the living-room floor, was, "Mummy's fallen." As if I were a child of four or five, or as if he were a little boy: *Mummy's fallen.*

"I'll be right there," I said, forgetting my promise to Pierce that I would stay clear of it. But this was the first time my father had ever needed me, so I said, without thinking, without wanting to think, "I'll be right there."

He was waiting for me. I could see him, as the taxi pulled into the driveway, standing behind the glass door. When I went inside, he said, "It's in there."

We walked across the foyer together, and at the archway into the living room I could make out a dark stain on the carpet. "There," he said, pointing to it. He explained that the glass she was carrying had broken beneath her.

There was a bottle of club soda on the coffee table. I'd seen him use it to get rid of various spills when I lived at home. I doubted that it would work on blood, but didn't say anything. Getting down on one knee, he poured some soda on the spot, and it fizzed as he talked.

"I thought at first that the house had been broken into, for Christ's sake," he said. "I called the police before I figured out what had happened."

He also had called an ambulance, which he followed to the hospital in his car. He told the nurses in the emergency department that she had tripped and had the wind knocked out of her, which was quick thinking, though of course they would not have believed it. Mum refused to let him see her after she'd been admitted, so he drove himself home, and called me.

When the soda had stopped bubbling I helped him up and put the kettle on for tea. Then I confessed. For Mum, for me, I told him of the promises we'd made six years ago, to protect him from the truth—so we both said.

"I walked into the kitchen one afternoon—it was the week before I left for university—and saw her putting a bottle under the sink," I began. "It was vodka, and it was half empty. And suddenly everything made sense to me. She said she had never been happy, and that she was killing herself slowly because she didn't have the guts to do anything drastic. But she said she would stop if I promised not to tell you. And then I moved out, and ... I didn't tell you."

What I didn't say was that I put it out of my mind, but that is exactly what I tried to do. I did not go home for visits very often, and jobs on campus kept me away all summer, too. When Mum called to check in with me (every Sunday at two o'clock sharp), Dad would shout in the background, "For crying out loud! It's long distance—do you want to put us in the poorhouse?" So we kept the calls short, which was fine with me.

"Dad?"

He did not look angry, which I had expected. And, very strangely, he did not appear to be surprised. *He must have known,* I thought, *he must have known all along.*

But he couldn't have known. No one could know that, and live with it, day in, day out, not for this long.

"Haven't you ever noticed how strange she becomes at night? The way she moves around the house?" It was true; when I lived at home she would glide through the rooms like a clumsy apparition, long after Dad had gone to bed. "She used to hand out extra allowance money to Gwen and me. We didn't ask, she just gave it."

I told him all of this, and more, but he was not listening. He was rubbing his hands together, waiting for me to finish. When I saw him not listening, I stopped. Because I realized then that the source of his calm was not knowledge, but disbelief; not comprehension, but dismissal. There was nothing left for me to say, or do.

"Leave it to me," he finally said. "I'll take care of Mummy now."

Mum was transferred to a private centre an hour away from the city, two days later. By the time I saw her, she had almost gotten over the tremors and the fury at having been taken anywhere in the first place. Sullenness had set in. The room didn't help: there was only a single bed, a veneer dresser with a mirror glued to the wall above it, and one vinyl and chrome office chair. The walls were pale grey.

"I didn't expect the room to be so spare," I said, hugging her. Her chin rested on my shoulder, though we are about the same height. She felt tiny and thin, fragile as a bird, in my arms. The smell of her took me back to early childhood, to rare hugs and to dressing up for Hallowe'en, when she would smear her Pond's cold cream all over my face so the makeup wouldn't stain my skin.

"Your father is supposed to bring me the yellow quilt," she said, releasing me. Her face looked puffy and was the colour of wholewheat bread batter. "You know, the one Besta made." Then, her voice breaking, "How is she?" I ran through answers she might accept. I didn't tell her about my visit to her mother, my grandmother, in the hospital the night before, just as I hadn't told Besta the truth about where Mum was.

"She's fine, don't worry!" I said. "I'll visit her more often for a while. She thinks you are here for exhaustion and she says that you deserve a rest. Which you do."

"Not in my wildest dreams did I ever think I'd end up in a place like this, Clara."

"I know. But it's not forever. You'll work through all this and go home again with a clean slate." I realized I was sounding like my father, and I pictured him saying this with a sweep of his arm, brushing it all aside as if it had no weight.

Suddenly she grabbed my arm with both hands. "Please get them to release me. I'll be fine, really. I'm so worried what your father is thinking. Please, Clara! I've learned my lesson ..."

"No, Mum. I can't do that," I said. She bit down on her teeth and said how cruel I'd become, she didn't *know* me, even, I was so cruel, that if Gwen were home this would never have happened, and that she'd never forgive me, not as long as she lived.

The next day Pierce was to drop me off at Dad's on his way to the university, where he was finishing his doctorate. (I had taken the practical route by becoming a librarian and getting a job to support us.) He was writing a thesis called "Bone Grammar: Sense and Sound in Modern Poetry," of which I knew very little. His demand for solitude and silence in those days was so familiar, so routine, that I mistook it as a condition of comfort. So I did leave him alone, as much as I could. I'd try to talk with him about his work at mealtimes, thinking he could use a little company and conversation, if only for a few minutes. I know I needed it.

That morning I'd seen his pyramid of spine-cracked books on the table, something by Eliot on top. "What is the point of poetry, anyhow?" I asked as I poured more coffee for him, and he answered, without missing a beat, "The complications of pleasure." This is the kind of thing I would miss the most about him, when we later parted: the easy flow of insights I could never come up with myself.

When I walked into the den, Dad was at his desk, holding the phone to his ear, but he wasn't speaking. His head was resting on the other hand, which supported his forehead and covered his eyes, and he was absolutely still. I had never seen him look so alone. I hadn't thought of how he might be feeling in that large, empty house.

I stepped back into the hallway, and called "Hello, Dad?"so he wouldn't know I'd seen him like that. He coughed and said, "Oh, hi, Clara," in his normal voice.

I invited him to dinner that night. Pierce wouldn't like it, but Dad was pleased.

I checked Mum's plants and found they were bone dry. Dad wouldn't think of watering them, so I got the pitcher from the cupboard under the sink and went about my task. I decided to take one to the clinic to cheer Mum's room. I chose a hardy geranium she'd taken in from the patio for the winter. A few petals lay scattered on the dusty sill, but it was still blooming, and a big red flower the colour of Besta's lipstick at the end of a firm stalk was reaching for the sun.

We knocked on her door and I let Dad go in first. As soon as I saw the room again I realized that he had forgotten to bring the quilt.

I showed the geranium to her, then put it on the dresser.

I was fearful, after yesterday's visit, of another round of recriminations, but Mum wasn't about to mention our conversation in front of Dad. She sat on the bed, arms at her side as if bracing herself.

"I've made a friend," she announced to us both, smiling.

Dad immediately stiffened, sniffed, and said, "What friend?"

"Marion, down the hall. She's been here longer than I have and she's explored the stores around town. I'm going shopping with her tomorrow."

"That's great, Mum," I offered.

Mum didn't have friends, not really, so I was surprised to hear her talk like this. She turned down most invitations to lunches and shopping and coffee, claiming that Besta needed her—a respectable enough excuse, though not true, or not the whole truth anyhow. It was Dad who would call through the house when Mum slipped off by herself. "Jenny? Jenny!" he'd shout up the spiral staircase. She'd reply with "I'm in the bathroom, Newman," which I used to think a shame until I found one, two, three bottles behind the Windex, under the vanity.

Dad had moved to the window and was rattling the change in his pockets.

"I'm going to the cafeteria for a minute," he announced,

and walked to the door. Then, fiddling with the handle, he said, "I hope you're safe in here, Jenny."

"Everyone here is very kind, Newman."

"Kind, sure, but *what* kind?" He looked at me, but I couldn't respond.

"Don't listen to him, Mum," I said after he had gone. "Of course you're safe."

"I know that. He's just worried. Do me a favour? Keep your eye on him while I'm in here?"

I was relieved, then, because she didn't ask me to sign her out. "While I'm in here" meant she would be staying, and would perhaps recover, and recover well.

So I said I would, of course I would, that Dad was coming to dinner tonight, in fact.

"Have you seen that huge dame at the cash register?" he asked when he came back in, chocolate bar in hand. The spaces between buttons on his shirt winked as he breathed hard from the stair climb. "People that fat should be shot!" he said.

Gwen and I used to laugh when he said this, this and things like it, when we were young. Later, when we were both in high school, Gwen nearly starved herself to death. When Dad heard her being sick in the bathroom one night, he was furious. "You wouldn't treat a dog the way you are treating yourself, young lady," he yelled, pounding on the door.

I remember that Mum, watching Gwen take pretend nibbles of dry toast at the breakfast table each morning, had had no reaction. She had given it all away years before, when Gwen's doctors said she probably wouldn't live to the age of six. Gwen lost half her weight and all of her hair, but the remission gave her a second chance. As far as we knew, she was still alive. She had left university in the middle of her third year (my first), and we hadn't heard from her since.

Dad ate his plate of stroganoff in half the time we did, so I dished out seconds for him.

"Why do you eat so fast?" I asked, knowing what he would say.

"Al-i-mentary, my dear, alimentary!" He and I laughed at his bad Sherlock Holmes. Dad thought Pierce didn't get it. "It goes back to my days as an intern," he explained. "You had ten minutes to wolf down your dinner, and it was the last you'd see for fifteen hours or more. So you made sure you got your fill, and fast."

I knew all this, of course, but I liked to see this side of my father—the one we'd get a glimpse of on a family vacation (for the last few days, before it ended), or on Christmas Day when he was not on call or making rounds. At those times, he made corny jokes and laughed at them, whether anyone else did or not; and he chatted with waiters, or on the phone, with an ease that was so unfamiliar that it drew Mum, Gwen and me together in a shy pleasure we knew would not last.

Tonight, though, his mood was forced. He was trying to be optimistic, and he was making an effort to be liked, which Pierce wouldn't realize, or wasn't going to respond to, if he did. Instead, making his usual excuses, he slipped away into the second bedroom we used as a study. Dad respected Pierce so much that he didn't seem to mind. Or perhaps he simply didn't notice.

I had offered a glass of wine earlier, though no one had been interested. When I poured myself a half glass now, Dad said, "Watch it, Clara. It might be in your genes, for crying out loud." I held my tongue. We talked about my job, about the role of the library in the history of civilization, about Dad's years at the University of Toronto, where Pierce was doing his degree now. It wasn't much, I know, but that night I felt as if my father and I were under a very sheer, shimmery fabric, both exposed to and sheltered from what had really gone on in the house all those years, from what was going on now. I thought, *I've never been so close to my father in my life.*

Pierce came out from under his books later to say goodnight. He shook my father's hand, and I kissed Dad's cheek.

"Well, better be off. I've got to get to the Sickhouse first thing in the morning."

"Sickhouse?" Pierce asked as I closed the door.

"The hospital. Sickhouse is his name for the hospital," I answered, and though I'd heard Dad say it all my life, it sounded odd to me when I repeated it to Pierce.

"It's called a kenning," Pierce explained, rubbing his chin. "I wonder if he knows that?"

"Probably. He harbours a dream of professorship. You remind him of him."

"God, really?" Then, "Your father is an interesting man." My future husband went back to his work, and I had dishes to do. But first, from the living room window, I watched Dad get into his white Oldsmobile, which he'd parked under the streetlight in front of our building. I kept watching as he drove away in the family-size car, slowly, in no hurry to get back to the twelve-room house and the well of his own company.

I'd forgotten to mention the quilt, so I called to leave a message. When the tape began I was startled to hear Mum. She was always so careful to sound cheery. I pictured my mother in that single bed at the Centre, while I listened to a voice that betrayed nothing: "We can't talk to you now, but please leave your name. One of the Morrows will call you tomorrow!"

I missed her. But I'd missed her for so long now; even before I left home, I had been missing her.

Dad never did take the quilt. Pierce said that he knew he wouldn't, that Dad deliberately "forgot" so that my mother wouldn't get too comfortable and not want to come home. I thought that was ridiculous, at the time, and we argued about it.

Nearly a year later, we got married and Pierce was hired to teach out west. Just before we moved away, we were invited to the house for dinner for the first time since Mum had been sent home.

Pierce parked his old Volvo station wagon next to Dad's car in the driveway, and through the front door I could see the chandelier sparkling in the foyer. Dad greeted us and seemed pleased that we had come. Mum was in the dining room, putting out the hand-embroidered tablecloth Besta had brought back from Norway.

We all sat in the living room. Dad filled four wine goblets and, holding his in the air, toasted: "To the young couple starting a new adventure. Bon Voyage, or as they say on the prairie, Bottled Water!"

At dinner, the table set with sterling silver cutlery and the gold-rimmed china, Dad opened a Cabernet to go with the meal. I was fairly quiet, but Pierce talked more that night than ever before. He told my parents how difficult it was for bibliophiles to let go of a single book, no matter what the moving cost might be. He told the story of his thesis defence, and Mum told about how anxious Dad had been while waiting for the results of his specialist exams.

"I hope you'll visit, once we find a place and settle in." It was unlikely that they would, and Pierce knew that, but he was excited about the move.

"We should go," I said after dessert. "I'd rather not be late for my last day at work."

I helped Mum clear the table, then splashed water on my face in the powder room. Pierce and Dad were already outside on the driveway. As I walked out of the house my mother touched my shoulder and said, "I'm all right, Clara. But if I'm not ... well, it's my life, not yours."

With that she put me back in my place, put up the glass wall that separated her and Dad from me, reminding me of the reach between who they were and what I wanted them to be. At that instant, I was devastated, naturally. But lately I've tried to think of it as her misguided sacrifice, that she did it to protect me rather than herself. Well. So much of happiness is in how you look at things.

Now I'm twenty-eight years old and Pierce has left me for one of his students, a nineteen-year-old with "the potential," he says, "to go places." Nothing complicated about that—it's as obvious as it gets. He called last week to ask how I was doing. I wanted to hang up, but I was lonely, and so we talked. He told me about his latest research, his colleagues, departmental politics; and I thought, had he always been so preening, and dull?

I'm still hoping for a call that will come not on a Sunday afternoon, but at some other day and time, a time when there will be no crisis or birthday or death or adultery. But I'm half afraid that it has already come, perhaps a long time ago, and I just didn't recognize it.

My mother has begun to communicate again, after a year or so of silence, calling when it's midnight in Ontario (nine o'clock for me). "I never get the time difference right!" she laughs, but I know that the only privacy she has is late in the evening, when Dad is asleep. Perhaps she feels badly for me (Besta would have told her of the separation); or perhaps, really, she is just as sad as she ever was. Tonight she is garrulous, sloppy.

"Too bad you are so far away. We can't even have lunch together, for goodness sakes! Remember the restaurants we went to?" she said last night, as if such outings had been a regular feature of life in Toronto—though really we went to the Danforth for Greek food together just the one time, and that was long before her collapse. To me it had seemed silly, as artificial as a first date, and I had described it to Pierce that way when I got home. Still, it must have meant something to her.

That lunch. We had souvlaki, and I pulled the lamb off the skewer one piece at a time as Mum talked about—what? The weather, no doubt, and Pierce, probably. That's right. And then she talked about her early days with Dad, I think. Yes—how he would tell her about his shift at the Toronto General, where he saw car accident victims and other catastrophies. There was the story where the daughter suffered severe head injuries after going through the windshield, her mother strapped into the driver's seat, watching it happen; and when Dad told the woman that her child was dead, all she could say was, "Oh, that's too bad." At the time of our lunch, Gwen was missing, hitchhiking to B.C., it turned out, and Mum wouldn't even say her name.

I wasn't sure why she told me the story that day, but perhaps it was an explanation of how she could let go of her children and spend a lifetime going alone through the motions of mother-love. Mentioning the lunch again during a long-distance call was perhaps as close as she might ever get to saying, *I had my reasons, for all of it; and I have my regrets, too.*

"Yes Mum," I say into the receiver. "I remember," but Dad must have woken up because she is gone.

III. Telling Besta

When I told Mac, my lover, the story about Besta's AIDs episode, he howled. It was true: when she was eighty-five, she convinced herself that she'd caught it from a cashier at the grocery store, someone with a ring in his ear who had sneezed on her change. It was not funny at the time, or not only, because she was serious; but Mac's listening made the sad seem lighter, somehow.

Oh, she could be difficult, and frustrating, and selfish, too, at times. "You are not as pretty as your sister, Little One," she said once, "but I like you best." I was eight years old, then. Later on, when I began to fill out a little, and a little too fast, she said straight out, "You should take some fat off." She had been known to faint when she was losing an argument, and she made more appointments to see our family physician than anyone in the history of his practice. For Besta, a red patch was a sure sign of lupus; constipation, a tumerous agony triggered by chemicals in the coffee or store-bought bread; nausea, nothing short of leukemia. Her medical vocabulary was precise, a proud catalogue of tongue-twisters in a Norwegian accent that was just as strong after fifty-five years in Canada as it had been the day she boarded ship: gallstones, phlebitis, cataract, colitis, hysterectomy, bronchitis.

Yes, she could be difficult. But I loved Besta—*bestemor*, best mother—for many reasons, not the least of which was that she let me.

When she died, three years ago—not long after Pierce left me—it was, as they say, from natural causes. I had just turned twenty-seven. That is an odd age, I know, to become an orphan, but the world at that time had become enormous, and I felt that I was disappearing on its surface.

I tried to explain some of this to Mac, who is a good listener. And I think I succeeded, at least in fits and starts. Mac never knew her, because we began our romance after Besta died; but he had been a true friend to me through my problems with Pierce, so I knew he would be patient with my tales, too. Leaning on his arm, stretched out long on the floor or on the bed, he knew when to ask a question and when he should let me be. And so we slipped into what became our odd kind of pillow talk.

*

I was home for Easter just before finals in my third year when I discovered that Besta was starting to fail. We were having tea in the living room of her apartment, but the cup she had given me was so dirty that I didn't want to drink from it. Besta had switched off "As the World Turns" especially for our visit. I had started to tell her about Pierce, whom I'd just met: that he was good-looking, of course, and blond, and that his hair was short; and yes, he was clean-shaven, most of the time. "And he is brilliant, Besta. He knows everything, and he's funny, too."

"When will you get married?" she asked, hoping, I think, that she would be going to a wedding in the summer—hoping she would have something to look forward to, somewhere to go where she could wear a hat and be known—the Grandmother, regal in a spotlight, important again. I dismissed her curiosity with a laugh and said marriage wasn't so important any more, though really I was just like her and thought nothing could be better than to have a husband and a home of my own.

Besta had been alone for five years by then. She should not have been living by herself any more; she could not see well enough to keep her apartment or herself clean. She asked me if, since I was there, I would mind helping her out of her cotton housedress so she could have a sponge bath without worrying about falling. Instead, I wiped out the tub, ran warm water into it, and helped her in.

"It's terrible to be old, terrible," she said, sitting down.

She did not seem to be bothered by my seeing her naked. She closed her eyes and raised her face to me so I could run the washcloth over it, and she lifted her arms to let me soap underneath them. I rung water out of the cloth over her rounded shoulders, her sagged breasts and her fleshy belly (she could eat plates of fattigmann cookies with her sugary tea). When I bathed her wide, dry back, she smiled, even though she was getting goose bumps by then. Afterwards I rubbed her dimpled, wrinkled body with a clean towel, and then I clipped her ragged toenails, which had softened some from the bath.

"Tank you, Clara. Still my girl," she said as I buttoned a blouse for her. "Just like your mother, always helping me."

When I went back to university, Besta sent frequent notes with yellowed return-address labels pasted on the back of the envelopes. She had cut out the words "Mr. and" so that "Mrs. Steinsväg" stood alone next to a neat rectangle of space. She would never have ordered new labels when so many were left in the desk drawer. I knew she mailed each letter on her way to the grocery store, where she ventured out to buy single lamb chops, small containers of orange juice, tea bags, a little gjetost and flat bread.

In more than one letter Besta asked why I thought my parents hadn't invited her to live with them. But I couldn't, or wouldn't, provide her with much of an answer. I thought, for instance, that I had heard my mother say on the night of my grandfather's funeral (after Besta had gone upstairs to sleep in our guestroom), "Why couldn't it have been *her*?"—but Mum's hands were covering her face, and I could be wrong about what she said. Dad barely spoke to Besta after that, except to reassure her that a freckle was a freckle and not melanoma; once, when Besta called Mum to complain of a pain in her stomach, he said, "Tell her she'll live to be a hundred, with our luck." So my reply to Besta's question, when I wrote back to her, would always be vague, something about my parents' busy schedule. I felt I was negotiating new territory with this, moving a little away from Besta and towards my mother, the instinct to protect—if that was what it was—shifting very slightly.

*

There was a waiting list at Carefree Lodge, but when Dad saw that Besta could no longer cope, he used his connections and had her moved in right away. Her corner room was one of the coveted singles. It had windows on two walls (each with a view of the garden), and the plush burgundy carpeting, elegant tone-on-tone wallpaper, and Victorian-styled light fixtures made the room welcoming. Mum brought in some of Besta's paintings, photographs and mementoes. It was really very nice, and Besta was grateful, and said so many times; but she knew that her place in the world had been reduced to a narrow bed, a television, an easy chair and the telephone. My father told her that she should count herself lucky, that at least she wasn't sharing an even smaller space with a stranger, like most of the residents. And that was true, as far as it went.

I visited her there on weekends when I was home from university, and then quite often when we moved back to Toronto so that Pierce could continue with his studies in graduate school. Besta was not happy that we lived together without being married, and she complained to me about it many times. But she knew she could get away with that kind of thing, with me.

The Lodge couldn't feed everyone at once, and Besta's was the early sitting for all three meals. Breakfast was at

7:00, so if she didn't want to go hungry all morning, she had to set her alarm for 6:15. The clock had been my grandfather's; he used to set it so that he would be up to chart the sunrise, the precise time of which he carefully recorded on a calendar from the bank that hung in the kitchen. Sunsets, too, were marked down, his guarantee of the next day's rise. He did this for years. After he died Besta kept his calendars in her dresser as if they were his diaries, and I suppose they were.

I usually went to see her in the afternoon, but sometimes, if I didn't plan it right, I'd arrive close enough to supper time that I would have to stay to walk her to the dining room. We'd set out twenty minutes ahead, Besta and I; she would wear her good brown shoes and carry her matching, empty, twenty-year-old purse on one arm, holding on to me with the other. Her mouth was set firm, and she looked straight ahead as we walked—pretending that she didn't mind being there, that she understood the necessity of it. It was hard to leave her there with the seven other men and women she would never try to get to know. She always asked me to stay, but guests were not allowed, so I would kiss her cheek and promise to come back soon and walk to my car without looking back.

I did like to help her get ready for these outings, though.

She would sit in her chair and I would stand behind her, easing the silver hairpins out without pulling. She would tell me stories about her mother tugging on matted manes with a comb made of ivory, and she would smile as I gently separated the long, thin strands with a soft brush. Then I'd braid it all over again, and pin it into a fresh coil around the top of her head, Scandinavian style, making a halo that would see her through the dinner hour. Silky white strands, as fine as the angel-hair clouds I remember gluing to blue construction paper in kindergarten, came loose in my hands. They had great roots at their ends that reminded me of pickled baby onions. Then she let me trace her lips lightly with the very red lipstick she had worn since the fifties.

When it became too difficult for Besta to dress and get to the dining room, even with help, her meals were brought in to her by the Carefree staff. They would place plastic-covered trays on the bureau and turn to leave, usually without a word.

These women also helped Besta to the bathroom, seated her and, afterwards, cleaned her. I was afraid of her new lightness (she'd lost so much weight!), and of her brittleness, afraid I would hurt her if I tried to help, and so I waited in the hallway. On her way back to bed I'd hear Besta say "Thank you very much" in her best English, careful to put her tongue between her teeth so as not to say "tank you," like she sometimes did, and that broke my heart.

*

When Mum was recuperating at the clinic, I told Besta that my parents had gone on a vacation, that Dad had surprised Mum for her birthday and taken her on a cruise. Besta said, "What about me?" and I told her I would come more often. I worked in shifts of three days on, one off, so it was easy enough to arrange. And my visits were enough, for a little while, but soon Besta was feeling abandoned and confused about how much time had passed. Apparently, between my days off, she slid into a black hole that she could not climb out of. The third day into it, the Lodge called (I was second on their emergency list) and asked if I could come, quickly. Besta had become hysterical, violent. "We can't tolerate that, you know," the administrator said on the phone. "They have to be able to live here in peace and quiet." So she had been taken to the hospital by ambulance. She fought the attendants, I was told, with strength that they could not believe.

When I found her on the geriatric ward, she was crying, and talking—in English—to one of her sisters, dead now for many years: "It's all my fault! She does too much for me! What have I done to her, Sigrid? What will I do without Mother?"

When I put my hand on her shoulder she shouted, "Don't touch me! Who are these men attacking me? Get me off this boat, it is terrible! *Yigh! Yigh! Aaaiiiyyy*—a version of the lullaby she used to sing to ease us into sleep, Gwen and me, when we were very young and wound up with the excitement of having her stay with us overnight.

By the time Besta had been calmed by sedatives, purple-green bruises already starting to show on her wrists where they'd tried to restrain her, it was dark. My father was at the clinic with Mum; Gwen was god-knows-where; and Pierce? I knew exactly where Pierce would be—just where he was when I got the call: at the library, ensconced in his carrel, filling notebook after notebook with words about words. So no one knew about Besta except me, and though I had been with her for hours, she had not yet recognized my face or my voice, or anything else about me. Besta had lived nearly ninety years, and who did she want now? Her mother, who had died of cancer when Besta was eleven years old.

I left the hospital and waited at the bus stop across the street. A hunched little woman hobbled down the sidewalk carrying three plastic grocery bags that overflowed with scraps of fabric and newspaper. She pulled a blue rag out of one and began to polish the bench, slowly. She rubbed in circles until the painted wood was gleaming in the shaft of street light, and then she curled up under the day's news.

Riding the bus home that night, I vowed that my life would be filled with many people, always. Not with children, necessarily, or with relatives, but with friends I would choose and who would choose me. They would be people who would not let me live out my days alone, and who would care about me and for me because they wanted to, and because I would do the same for them. At that point I didn't have anything like that in my life, not really, but I was glad that I'd seen the need for it before it was too late.

A few months later, when Mum was home and Besta was back at the Lodge, Pierce married me. That was how it seemed; we did not marry, he married me—and then, a month after that, we were getting ready to move to Saskatoon, where he was to teach at the university. And there came the day when I could not put it off any longer, so I drove out to see Besta. It was in early evening and she was already in bed, though the lights were on and she was not asleep. We talked for a while, and when she was getting tired and I had to go, I could not say goodbye. The word would not come. It simply wouldn't. I said "I love you," instead.

"I'm glad someone does," she said. "Well, have a good life, Little One, and keep in good humour with your husband. Just be yourself. No babies is a good idea. Tings change when they come. If only Einar was here, I would give anyting. Anyting ..." and she fell into sleep.

*

A few days after Besta died, a package arrived from my mother. Inside were all the weekly letters that I had sent to Besta over the year. I had no idea that Mum had saved them, and I am still not sure why she did. I knew that she had probably seen them, on Thursday afternoons, because Besta would have wanted her to read them out loud. It would give them something to talk about. I thought of this scenario every time I wrote to her, but I don't think it changed what I said, or how I said it. In Mum's note—the first since we moved away—she said, "In the end she didn't know her own name. Or yours either, of course."

So I had lost Besta months before her actual death, then. The Besta I'd written to—the charmer who used to ask after Pierce, who would pretend to flirt with him when we visited ("are you jealous, Little One?"); the friend who would touch my new dress and ask, "Is it cotton?" and "How much did it cost?"—that Besta had, bit by bit, turned away from the world of days and hours and turned back to another kind of time, cloud-time. She had drifted away, and the world felt emptier for it, very empty, and very dark.

I re-read every one of my letters. The early ones were filled with optimism and descriptions of the small house Pierce and I had found when we arrived on the prairie. I told her about the funny-shaped rooms, and how we'd arranged the furniture in them; about the neglected back yard, and the neighbours we'd met. I wrote about the part-time position I'd taken at the library, which was dull, and about the parties Pierce's colleagues invited us to, which were not. I tried to answer questions she might have about our new lives so far away, and so I explained what were, to me, the oddities of the place: in summer, the boldness of the unrelentingly open sky; in winter, cars locked and left running outside shopping malls and restaurants. I told her the joke we heard over and over: "They say it gets so cold here that you're charged with attempted murder if you pass a hitch-hiker without stopping!"

Gradually, the letters became muted and tired. I hadn't realized I had been so down, so soon, or that—when I did know—I had stopped sharing my daily life with Besta. I said very little that was real. I wasn't myself, not the person she had known. The person she knew would have confided in her about Pierce, and wished for advice, but in my letters I had become guarded, hurried. No wonder she couldn't remember my name.

For days afterwards, I made cup after cup of tea the way Besta had liked it (five teaspoons of sugar; she could not be fooled by three), and felt shipwrecked. I took time off work. I ate very little of anything, then worked my way through bags of cookies and potato chips, and whatever I could get at the corner store. I slept for hours during the day, and then could not rest all night. Sometimes, in the dark, I found myself humming Besta's lullaby—"*a-yigh, yigh, yigh; a-yigh, yigh, yigh*"—a sentence of wordless bars in a minor key that tells an entire life story, one of youth and love and exile and betrayal and family and old age. And loneliness. It is a plainsong of loneliness.

*

I didn't go to the funeral. On my salary alone, I couldn't afford the flight, but I was in no shape to face my family anyway. No, I couldn't have flown home. What I did was this: I collected all the photographs I had of Besta and fanned them out. A smiling young girl standing next to her unsmiling parents. A teenager sitting in a row with her six smocked sisters. A shy young woman leaning on the arm of her fiancé, her wild eyes sparkling like moonstones. Christmas in Sudbury, with Mum and Uncle Leif by the tree. The retirement photo in the Inco Newsletter, her hair cut short and permed and strange. Propped up in her bed at the Lodge, the nurse's sign posted above: "DO NOT PUT ON LEFT SIDE."

I looked at all of these, and I thought about Besta asking me as I combed her hair if I believed in heaven. I had answered by shaking my head and saying, "I don't know." I was newly in love, and impatient with her sorrows that day. But I wish I'd said "Yes! There are many heavens, Besta. Remember in the *Edda*? It says that one heaven is fiery and jewelled, and another is higher than the clouds, beyond all tears. They will be waiting for you there ..."

Eventually, my mother and I became friends again. No, I shouldn't say "again"; we became friends for the first time, really. We began listening to each other, and we even started to talk about Besta. When Mum told one of her stories, she had a fondness in her voice that I've rarely heard: "She never got over her mother dying, you know. And the woman wasn't kind, not at all. She was so severe that Besta wouldn't want to sit down for days after one of her scoldings, the poor thing. How she could love her so much, I don't know." She told me about the newly married Besta and the tiny household she set up in small-town Ontario—about the outsider with a funny accent, who earned extra for the clothes she loved to buy by polishing silverware for the wives of the Inco elite. And she told me about the time Besta dressed up in her good suit for a doctor's appointment, saying to her ten-year-old that she wouldn't be coming home, no, she wouldn't, not this time.

I repeated Mum's stories to Mac, carefully, as though I were folding egg whites into a cake—not knowing how it all blends together, exactly, but trusting that it would turn into something else, something both rich and light. And I began to realize, in this telling, that Mum has always carried Besta's grief in her heart, and that her love for Besta was not less than or even equal to mine, but of a different order altogether.

*

Tonight the Saskatoon sky is lush with a light that seems to come from no earthly source, bathing the length of my street, and all of our small wooden houses, in a wash of pink that hints at some pleasure I can't recall. Even the garage behind the house, with its peeling yellow paint, and the neighbour's knocked-about garbage bins, and the soggy mattress that's leaned for a year against the electrical pole—these, too, have become unfamiliar and extraordinary in this diffuse glow of late afternoon.

My own house, I have worked on from the outside, in.

The long and narrow grassy patch that is the extent of my backyard is now rimmed with flowers: seas of pansies, day lilies and marigolds, amazing sunflowers taller than me. Between the rows, in the centre of the plot, I have made a small berm. Rocks fringe it, and thyme and alyssum creep among caned delphiniums and astilbe. In the shade of the house, ferns uncurl over a sweet mulch of pine.

This summer the house was revived with a fresh coat of sage green. Mac and I painted it together, on weekends and after work, and a couple of times we turned on the porch lights and painted at night. Inside, too, there are bursts of colour: teal and blue, downstairs, and pumpkin yellow (Mac calls it papaya) for my bedroom. There is a lot to be done, still—plastering walls, refinishing floors; the kind of work I've never done before—but, with Mac's help, it should be fine, more than fine. You see, I've had to learn joy, to trust the surprise of it, and to linger inside it as long as possible.

No, we're not finished yet, and I don't mind at all.

Acknowledgements

My sincere thanks to editor Lynn Henry for her commitment to the stories; to Dr. Donald S. Hair, professor and mentor, who encouraged me to choose a writer's life; and most of all, always, to G.K. Betts, without whom *Stubborn Bones* and so much else would not have come into being.

About the Author

Karen Smythe's short stories have appeared in numerous literary journals. Her critical study of Mavis Gallant and Alice Munro, *Figuring Grief: Gallant, Munro and the Poetics of Elegy* (McGill-Queen's Univerity Press), was published in 1992. She has lived in Winnipeg, Toronto, Regina and Halifax, and now resides near Wolfville, Nova Scotia.